Wide Open

Chronicling the Manic Misadventures of Dr. Dee and Her Return to Sanity

Denise B.

PublishAmerica
Baltimore

© 2007 by Denise B.
All rights reserved. No part of this book may be reproduced, stored in a retrieval system or transmitted in any form or by any means without the prior written permission of the publishers, except by a reviewer who may quote brief passages in a review to be printed in a newspaper, magazine or journal.

First printing

"Part Three" of this book is a work of fiction. Names, characters, places, and incidents either are the product of the author's imagination or are used fictitiously. Any resemblance to actual persons, living or dead, events, or locales is entirely coincidental.

ISBN: 1-60441-448-0
PUBLISHED BY PUBLISHAMERICA, LLLP
www.publishamerica.com
Baltimore

Printed in the United States of America

The excerpts from *Alcoholics Anonymous* are reprinted with permission of Alcoholics Anonymous World Services, Inc. (AAWS) Permission to reprint these excerpts does not mean that AAWS necessarily agrees with the views expressed herein. A.A. is a program of recovery from alcoholism *only*. Use of these excerpts in connection with programs and activities which are patterned after A.A. but which address other problems or in any other non A.A. context does not imply otherwise.

Excerpt from *Mrs. Dalloway* by Virginia Woolf, copyright 1925 by Harcourt, Inc. and renewed 1953 by Leonard Woolf, reprinted by permission of the publisher.

To Marion

to NAMI Tennessee ~
happy Reading ~
Denise B.

PART ONE
Mania Firsthand

Chapter One

Euphoria! Creativity! Superhuman powers! Such are the lures of the manic state.

For eleven years I trudged along, building a sober, happy, productive life. In that time, I returned to college teaching, developed solid relationships with family and friends, became part of a writers' workshop and composed a book and several essays, of which the latter were published. Active in AA and church, I was happy and fulfilled.

Then one day I simply decided to stop taking my medication. At the time I was on Paxil, an anti-depressant, prescribed several years before due to a summer of profound depression in which I was in constant anxiety over finding enough work and just wanted to sleep all the time. But that depression, I told myself, was long gone. In fact, I was beginning to feel a beautiful, natural high.

I was also taking Zyprexa, an anti-hallucinogen, which had been prescribed when I'd suffered the hallucination that people were crouching outside my bedroom window, talking about and jeering at me. My new doctor had said that he planned to wean me off the Zyprexa, and I thought I'd take matters into my own hands and just quit cold turkey. I didn't consult him about my decision or tell him about this newfound sense of euphoria. I was afraid that if I said something, he'd prescribe a medication to take it away. Indeed, he probably would have diagnosed the early stages of mania. But I was not taking that chance. As an undiagnosed manic depressive, I only knew that I felt really, really good. (I now know that it is likely that the antidepressant probably tipped me over into a manic state.)

I noticed surges of elation. I had new energy, lots of it. At the time, I was teaching English at the community college level; it was the start of fall semester. I had difficulty teaching. When I was in front of the class, it felt as if I were expanding out of my skin. My thoughts were flying loose, and it was very difficult to focus. I was on sensory overload: all sensations seemed to be rushing in at me. Hence, I felt "wide open."

I reasoned this situation out and decided it would be good for me to quit all my teaching jobs. After all, they had no prestige. I'd been trained to teach at the university level. Why not take a break, live on my savings, and then go for a university position in the new year? Surely Harvard, Princeton, and Yale would offer me a job once they realized how important I was. At the time, I was teaching at two community colleges. With glee, I resigned from both.

Being free during the day was delightful. For years, I'd wanted to write a play called *Wheels*, using as its theme John Lennon's song of that name. I also intended an allusion to Ezekiel's "wheels within wheels." It was to be a spiritual allegory. I got started. To my amazement, the play practically wrote itself. My fingers flew on the keyboard. I found that I needed very little sleep, and I devoted all my time to it. Within weeks, it was complete.

I would produce it and take it on the road, I decided. I made up business cards reading "TROUPE: Dr. Dee, prop." I had decided to change my name to Dr. Dee. It was a play on my first initial and it hearkened back to John Dee, the Elizabethan mathematician who believed he had the alchemical secret of turning metal into gold.

Now to cast it. I needed a man and woman to play the masculine and feminine aspects of God; a divine dog and cat; Satan and his female consort; a troupe of traveling troubadours consisting of Mary Magdalene, Saint Paul, a nun, and a fool; a man and a woman up for judgement. I recruited people from a 12-step clubhouse and other AA meetings and set up a rehearsal schedule. Of the people I'd recruited, three wanted to be paid. No problem! I had a healthy savings account. Anyway, I figured, soon the play would pay for itself. After a big first night in South Pasadena, I'd take the play on the road (appropriate, given the title), recruit local talent in each new town, and present it again and again. Key characters in the play comprised a troupe of traveling troubadours. Thus, to have a traveling production only made sense.

At the 12-step clubhouse I also found a couple of men who were living right outside in an abandoned car. They were eager to join the troupe, so I made them in charge of sound (it was to be a musical) and lighting. Since we were all free during the day, they became my production assistants and I gave them cash when they needed it.

One day at the clubhouse another man approached me. His car had been impounded and had accumulated tickets as well. If I would bail out the car, he'd let me use it for a month. Sounded like a good deal to me. *Wheels* needed wheels, right? My production assistants could use a car. As I was driving around to the bank, the police station, the impound yard, Lennon's song "Wheels" came on the radio. Perfect! A sign from God that I was on the right track.

As director, I was very strict. No one could miss more than three rehearsals without being booted from the cast. When a member of the cast stumbled over the verse script, I would stop rehearsal and make him/her repeat the lines until they were perfect. There was, predictably enough, a high dropout rate. The cast was composed of amateurs who had expected a lighthearted, fun production. I was making the whole experience very intense, and they grew afraid of me. Each time someone quit, I would go back to the 12-step clubhouse and recruit a newcomer.

At dress rehearsal, before we got started, I began a public diatribe against the sound man and lighting man. I ranted and raved against them, focusing on their carelessness over the car I had bought for their use and which had been impounded again because it had broken down.

I accused them of stealing the car and threatened them with the police. Both left, indeed went running out, and many in the cast also left that night, one star performer telling me that she couldn't work under my direction any more:

"I can't do it! This project was supposed to be fun, and instead you give out a strong negative energy. I can't stand to be around it."

On the day of our first performance, I had scheduled a final rehearsal. A few diehards showed up. I was stern and dictatorial. They all left but one, who had been a friend. What to do? A play scheduled and no cast. I looked at the clock. Still a few hours to go before show time. I began to run through the various parts myself. My friend left, commenting, "I didn't know it was to be a one-woman show."

Undeterred, I went to the closets of the Women's Club, the place I had rented for the first performance. There I found many mops and brooms. I began to dress each mop and broom by fastening a wire coat hanger around it to serve as shoulders and head. Over each head, I placed a hat or crown. I draped the costumes on the frames. I then propped my "characters" onstage and got myself ready.

That night, the audience consisted of my mother, two woman friends, a man from my church, and a reviewer from a small local paper. I came onstage, explained that the cast had fled but that the show must go on, and proceeded with the play, reading each part while holding the appropriate costumed broom or mop. Later I learned that the reviewer had commented, "That was the bravest thing I have ever seen."

After the play, I fell apart. Everyone had deserted me! No one came to the play! I was devastated. My pastor came to visit me and I dissolved in tears, vowing to quit all twelve-step programs because they had betrayed me. I asked him if I could regroup by working in the area behind the church kitchen, outdoors, where there was a long table. He readily agreed.

Days I spent behind the church, drawing and making increasingly incoherent documents and playing with the costumes I'd retrieved from the performance. Nights I spent at a 24-hour coffee shop, trolling for bums. I had decided that my new ministry would be helping the homeless. I would call my ministry "Heart." Whenever I was asked for spare change, I would offer to buy the person a meal and then take him/her to a nearby motel to spend the night. Did not the Bible tell us to give when asked?

WIDE OPEN

I was unconcerned about how much this activity, on top of what I'd spent on the play, was costing me. To my mind, the money supply was endless. All my needs, I was sure, would be met by God. And I was divinely inspired, an emissary of God. I could do no wrong.

One day I was going through the mail that I had let accumulate while I had been absorbed by the play, and I came across a self-addressed, stamped envelope. I'd written a book on my years as a homeless alcoholic and had enclosed such envelopes with copies of the manuscript when I mailed them to publishers. I'd gotten many rejection slips in response and, certain that this would be another, had tossed it to one side unopened.

Upon opening it now, I was amazed to read: "We find your manuscript interesting and intriguing and would like to publish it in hardcover...our authors must be willing to use their real names and to do publicity events as they come up...our offer is valid for ten days following receipt of this letter."

Someone wanted the book! I checked the date on the letter; ten days had passed. I quickly called the press to explain that I'd been busy producing a play and that I did indeed want to accept the offer. The woman I spoke with was encouraging and reiterated that the press would be launching a major publicity campaign, to which I readily agreed.

One afternoon while I was playing behind the church, I looked up and in amazement saw my family emerge from a car. There was my brother from the Bay Area, my sister from San Jose, my daughter from Hollywood. They asked me to please accompany them to my mother's house, where I was living at the time.

"I'm quite busy now," I told them. "It was nice of you to come for a visit, but I've got things to do here. Important things."

"Just take a little break," they implored. "Come have some lunch. We're just here to help."

They gave me lunch from MacDonald's (no fries—they had eaten them, I noted glumly) and took me into the den, where I had spread out a Day of the Dead table with candles and pictures of relatives who had died. They were puzzled by the display but did not let it distract them from a showdown. They had come at my mother's behest to intervene.

DENISE B.

They told me my behavior was unacceptable. I'd quit work, I was up all hours, my mood swings were frightening to my mother. My daughter told me I'd ruined her childhood through years of alcoholism and that now she was afraid she'd lose me again. My brother told me I was being selfish and hurting our mother. My sister, very calmly and persistently, asked me to go to the psychiatrist and get help.

Finally, to shut them up, I agreed to go to the doctor if they would accompany me so that we could have a family meeting with him. I expected that the doctor would take my side and dissuade them from interfering with my life. They agreed to come along.

My brother drove, but he seemed to be going the wrong way. My daughter directed him to a hospital instead of to the doctor's office. I was baffled. Once at the hospital, there was a long wait. Bored, I began to wander. I decided that I had super healing power, and that all patients I looked at with my healing eyes would be cured. I told the people at the desk, "I am a good doctor myself, Dr. Dee in the flesh! I do not need another doctor. I'll heal myself and all the others who are waiting here."

Finally a psychiatrist arrived. She quickly diagnosed me as bipolar (manic depressive), in a manic phase. She brought a shot of something with her, which I declined to take. She told me, "You either take the shot now, or you get strapped to a stretcher and you'll be forced to take the shot." I submitted. To my horror, I was strapped to a stretcher anyway. I was filled with shock and a strong sense of betrayal. The doctor had tricked me. My family had tricked me, too.

"Why are you doing this to me?" I cried out to my family piteously.

"We think it's for the best," my daughter replied calmly. And off I went.

I was taken to a small mental health facility near Chinatown in Los Angeles. All my property was bagged and tagged, and I was told there was no smoking, not even outside in the patio. I was disgusted. This was some awful mess my family had gotten me into.

That night I barely slept. By a hall light, I read a pamphlet on patients' rights that I found in the room. I discovered there that I was entitled to representation and that no one could force me to take medication I did not want. Armed with that information, I began to plot my escape.

The next morning, I refused all medication. I attempted to contact an organization mentioned in the pamphlet, but only got a recording. My mother, daughter, sister, and a friend came to visit. When I saw them, I was livid with anger. They had put me here against my will! I lashed out at them all.

"You're the scum of the earth! Curses be upon you! You've deprived me of my human rights through a cheap trick. I never want to see you again, and as for you, my daughter, I disown you."

Saddened, they left me alone.

I stayed about a week in the mental health facility. I finally realized that in order to get out, I would have to behave in an extraordinarily calm and sane manner. That, I decided, I could fake. When it was time for me to be interviewed by a doctor, I drew on my inner resources and pulled up my professional persona. I explained to her that I had quit my jobs because I fully intended to pursue a career as a university professor, a job for which I was qualified. I told her I thought that I, not my family, was the one to decide on my career plans. I also told her that the reason I'd refused medication was that it was not being prescribed by my own doctor, who was the one who knew my case history.

I convinced her. I was released. With another huge surge of elation, I took a cab to Chinatown, where I asked the driver to take me to the Bank of America and then to a motel. I paid him off, booked a room, and was all set for a new adventure.

I knew it would be expensive to have an interlude in Chinatown, but I decided I would keep track of all expenses and bill my family. After all, they were the reason I'd ended up in the loony bin, and now I deserved a vacation.

In Chinatown, I went on a huge spending spree. Each morning, I'd go to the bank and draw out a hundred or two in cash. Then I'd hit the stores and buy whatever appealed to me: a statue of Buddha, a new hat, a new shawl, nesting bowls, jewelry—purchases, purchases.

My appearance was flamboyant, to say the least. I dressed in lots of bright colors, always with a hat. I bought magic markers and would decorate my face with them, drawing a heart (for my ministry Heart) and a cross (to show I was a missionary) on my cheeks.

When I wasn't buying, I was cruising the streets in the neighborhood looking for homeless people to help. Once I found an encampment, and I put several twenties under a rock nearby. Once I found a homeless fellow sitting on a curb. He asked about the cross around my neck (I had taken to wearing a huge cross). I gave it to him, bought him food, gave him enough for a motel room, and called him a cab. (No doubt, when I left he walked away and spent the money for what he wanted, wine or drugs).

Remembering my book offer and concerned that my new publisher would have had no way to contact me, I phoned her from the motel to give her their fax number so that she could send a new contract. I explained that I was working now from the motel.

"I'm engaged in a ministry for the homeless, and all my money is going into it, and all proceeds from the book will go to help the homeless too."

She sounded very dubious. "Well, that's very nice of you, but…"

We hung up without firming up the contract, but I was sure she'd see things my way and soon fax one over.

I had a marvelous time in Chinatown, pretending to be a wealthy eccentric. I scouted for locations for a theater I could buy, figuring that I could use my IRA savings for a down payment and that God would provide the rest. That way, I could keep producing new versions of *Wheels*.

Finally, though, I began to miss my car. I would have to risk a trip home to collect it. I could say my final farewells to the family and hit the road. I took a cab from Los Angeles to South Pasadena and, with some trepidation, approached the condo building where I had been living with my mother for the past few years.

As I was approaching, the condo manager was coming out. He was delighted to see me. He explained that the locks had been changed on the building, and that my mother and family had been very concerned about me. Mom was away, visiting my sister in San Jose for Thanksgiving, but she had asked him to let me in if I should show up. That was a big relief to me. I'd be able to go in, retrieve the car, and leave without any family visit at all. Family, after all, was my enemy. They were the ones who had put me away against my will.

Rudy, the manager, invited me to lunch. Why not? He drove us to a nearby restaurant and we ordered. Then, to my disgust, he began lecturing me on the importance of family. "You need to realize how lucky you are to have a family that cares about you. My family is gone. Both my parents are dead. Yours loves you and wants the very best for you."

I was unable to sit still. "My family is a group of traitors who tricked me and trapped me," I hissed. "I'm going to get out of here before they can do it again. Give me the keys." He hesitated. "Give me the keys!" I shouted. To avoid a scene, he did. I got up, left him sitting there stunned, and walked home. On the way I began proclaiming in a loud voice an improvised speech on human rights and how mine had been violated.

Once at the condo, I began a frantic search for my car keys. They were nowhere to be found. I called my sister in San Jose. I cut off her questions about my welfare.

"You're a traitor! You infringed my human rights! I'll never forgive you. I just need one thing: where are my car keys?"

She began to cry and put my mother on the line. Mom remained calm through my ranting. She was vague about the location of my keys, but assured me that both she and my sister would be back the day after Thanksgiving and we would resolve everything then. I hung up on her.

I had a few days alone at the condo. I had a couple of strong fantasies going that were, I was convinced, very real. One involved what I called "The Chain of Command." On top were God, Christ, and the Holy Spirit. Next came me and Mary Magdalene, equal partners. Below us came the apostles, and below them the saints. The Chain of Command gave me a lot of power, and I could feel it coursing through my body constantly.

DENISE B.

Since I slept very little I often walked to a 24-hour coffee shop nearby and, after filling up on caffeine, would step outside to smoke and pace, repeating "The Chain of Command" over and over and marking it out with my feet on the pavement. One time I was still there in the morning and met an elder of my church who was going in to breakfast.

"How are you doing?" he asked, concerned. "We haven't seen you in church."

"I do not need church these days," I countered. "Anyway, who are you to question me? I outrank you!"

The second fantasy involved a specific job, soul doctor. My role was to prepare the souls who had died to meet their Maker. It was up to me to decide who was going to Heaven, who to Hell. Once the decision was made, I prepared a Soul Boat and sent them on their way. A Soul Boat was sometimes drawn on paper, sometimes written in words, and sometimes created out of found objects.

On Thanksgiving Day I decided that the souls in my charge needed a cleansing ritual. I hooked up a long hose to a sink in the condo and stretched it out so that it was aimed over the side of the patio. (Our condo was on the second floor). The water gushed out, and I was very pleased. Cleansing was important.

I said ritual prayers and then left the water flowing to go into the study and prepare more Soul Boats, constructing them on the computer. I also used the word processing program to fight off enemy forces who were trying to invade my mind. I was deeply engrossed in my work when, with a jolt, I realized that there were people in the condo. Invaders!

"It's okay, Rudy, I've got the water turned off," said a neighbor. Rudy himself came into the study. He tried to explain that the water had been flooding into the patio of the unit beneath me. I barely registered his words. I was badly shaken by what seemed to be a major violation of my sacred space.

"Get out!" I shrieked. "Get out now, both of you!"

They left. I remained shaken and aghast. The sanctity of my important work had been breached. I had to perform a ritual to build up my wall of privacy again. I searched for something I could use and found a paper eagle in red, white and blue, a decoration for the Fourth of July. Perfect. Symbol of human rights. I lit a match and burned it. True, it started a small fire in the den, but I was able to quickly put it out. Now I had symbolized what had occurred: total violation of human rights. Now I was restored.

The intercom buzzer sounded. Who could it be? I pressed the button for speaker phone. "It's Jessica and Sacha. Please let us in, Mom." Ha! As if I could be tricked that easily! I knew what my daughter and her husband wanted. It could only be to lock me up again. I told her to go away and made sure the doors were all locked.

I made it through Thanksgiving but soon discovered that I had a problem with cash flow. There was a check from one of my schools in the mailbox, but I could not cash it. Why not? Back in Chinatown, I had become convinced that I needed to rid myself of all my material possessions. When Christ sent his disciples out to evangelize, after all, he told them to bring nothing with them: no cash purse, no change of clothes, no extra staff. So I had gone out to the pavement, dragging all my purchases in a little cart I had brought, and set them all out as a display. While I was at it, I went through my wallet and left, on top of the pile, my bank card, my maxed out credit card, and my license. I had walked away, feeling cleansed.

Now, however, it was a problem. I couldn't cash the check without proper I.D. or bank card. I needed cigarettes and food. What to do? I went around to local merchants, presented my paycheck, and tried to get them to cash it. No go. I went to my church, and tried to get my pastor to cash it. No go. Not only was he unwilling to give me cash, he wanted me to contact my family. I sensed danger. He was on their side and wanted to see me locked up again. I left as quickly as I could.

I finally went to our local Mexican restaurant, where Mom and I had had dinner every Wednesday night for years. I reminded them that I was a loyal customer but was embarrassed to be temporarily out of cash. Would they help? They considered, and gave me a take-out order. When I got it home, I discovered it was only a container of salsa and a bag of tortilla chips. Chintzy! Nevertheless, I ate it.

DENISE B.

The next day, my mother and sister arrived. I demanded that they give me cash and car keys. Mom gave me a twenty, but said she'd have to hunt for the keys. I left for the local Macdonald's, stopping on the way for cigarettes, and had coffee and a smoke. Upon my return, I confronted them again. My sister had the keys. She held them in her hand. But she was blocking the door.

"I'll give them to you after you come with us to see your doctor," she said.

I was enraged. I went to attack her. My mother pulled me off, and I shoved her away. I went for my sister again. I kicked her in the stomach and lunged to bite her. She gave me the keys and I ran out the door.

I drove aimlessly before deciding that I would have to return one last time to pack up the car with whatever clothes and goods I would need for my road trip. When I returned, my sister was waiting with a restraining order. I was to have no contact with either of them, and I was not to return to the condo.

"Good! I'll never be back, you traitors!"

She had brought out some of my clothing and gave me a little cash. I was surly. "You can certainly afford it, you rich bitch."

She cried. I packed up the car. She tried to hug me goodbye, but I pushed her away and took off. I had no glasses, I had no license, but that did not bother me. Off I went.

Chapter Two

That night I parked in a strange neighborhood and crawled into the backseat. I used clothing as a pillow and my coat as a blanket, and I slept. In the morning, I was filled with exhilaration. I was free. I would begin my new ministry, Heart. I pointed the car out of town and drove, undeterred by the fact that without my glasses I could not really read road signs, ending up in downtown Los Angeles.

I began hunting for homeless people and found some. Along with my own clothing, I had in the car trunk some belongings of a cast member who had asked me to store them. Among them I found a toiletries kit, shoes, blankets. These I gave away.

I made it to a coffee and donut shop and there, outside, was approached by a young black man who asked me for change. I offered to buy him a coffee and donut. We went inside and talked.

"So tell me about yourself," he began.

"Well! I'm a woman with two jobs. I run a ministry called Heart to help the homeless. I'm also a theatrical producer with a new play out, and I'm currently looking for property to open a theater. I'll be needing local talent."

"Why, that's great. I'm a writer myself."

"Marvelous! I can use you."

"There's only one thing. I'm about to be evicted from my room because I can't pay the rent. I wonder if you could help?"

How fortunate I was. Here was new talent and a chance to use the ministry, two in one. I drove him to a residential district. He directed me to a house that had an outbuilding behind it.

DENISE B.

"My landlady lives in front, and I live in a room in the back."

"Let's talk with her. I don't have any more cash, but we can do something."

The landlady was skeptical until, hunting through my belongings, I discovered that my sister had included a box containing a checkbook and bank statements along with a new credit card that had come in the mail. I wrote her a check for my new friend's back rent and offered her my one remaining credit card to buy groceries. She was pleased and offered me a room.

"You can stay here with us. We provide meals, and I'll make sure you take your meds."

I was insulted. What did she mean, meds? Was I behaving like a person on meds? She was gravely mistaken. However, I'd take her up on her offer of temporary lodging.

I then learned that, just as people were renting from her, she was renting the entire property. Her own landlord came to collect. I approached him and made my pitch.

"I'm a theatrical producer looking to buy property. I wonder if you could help me find something appropriate."

"Of course. I have some buildings you could look at."

"Excellent. In the meantime, I wonder if you could help me out with cash flow. I have lost my driver's license and bank card. My purse was stolen. If I write you a check, could you cash it?"

"As long as it's under fifty dollars, I will."

I wrote him a check for forty, he cashed it, and I felt secure again. We made an appointment for the following morning so that he could show me property.

I felt an urgent need to get my affairs in order. While the landlady left to go grocery shopping, I took the box of bank statements and set it in the living room of the outbuilding. While my new friend watched, I carefully went through the statements and balanced my checkbook. I was pleased to discover that I was still solvent. Leaving everything carefully arranged, I went out to the porch for a cigarette.

I relaxed in the sun on the porch. This was a good new beginning. Soon I'd cash in my IRA and start the theater up again. Life was wonderful. Time to unpack the car. I went for an armload of clothing and returned to the outbuilding. What was this? My carefully arranged bank statements had been hastily gone through and lay in a messy pile. My checkbook was gone. It was chaos on the floor. My new friend was missing. I had been robbed!

I was filled with self-righteous anger. I rang the landlady's bell. She was still gone. We'd agreed to go dancing that evening, but she was still gone. What to do, what to do. I waited on the porch, seething. I paced the street where my car was parked. Finally she returned. But instead of being pleasant, she was demanding.

"What are you doing out in the cold with no coat? Give me your car keys now."

Another traitor. There was no time to lose. I turned and quickly sped off on foot. I ran through streets that twisted and turned, across railroad tracks, deep into a foreign neighborhood, until I came to a small bar. Safe haven.

Well, I had planned to go dancing and dance I would. I ordered a beer and loaded the jukebox with songs I liked. I drank and danced by myself, enjoying the freedom. From time to time I would go out back to have a cigarette and to urinate. I played with the shadows on the wall, and I admired the strange shapes my urine made in the dust. Each shape, I decided, represented a country I would conquer.

Finally it was late, my money was gone, and I figured it was safe to go back and retrieve my car. I would slip away while they all slept. Then I would return in the morning with a policeman and retrieve my checkbook and credit card. I trudged along, trying to backtrack. It was all strange terrain. I started to go in circles. The house had a tree in front, so I looked for a tree. Nothing. No house, no tree, no car. It got later and later, colder and colder. I kept walking, knowing I was lost but not knowing what else to do.

I was bitterly cold now. A van slowed to follow me, and then stopped. The Hispanic driver reached over and opened the passenger door.

"Frio?"

"Si."

"Come. You come. Warm here."

Gratefully, I climbed in the back of the van. He got in back with me and indicated that I was to take my pants off. In a mix of Spanish and English, I declined, saying I was a bride of Christ and could not break my vows. Since I had embraced celibacy for eleven years, I decided I had become a lay sister.

He loomed over me. "I keel you."

"Then kill me."

I closed my eyes, fully prepared to die. I was calm. Would he use a knife? A gun? It mattered little. Soon I would be face to face with Christ. Instead, I felt him tugging my pants down and I gave in.

It was soon morning. The driver gave me some money and dropped me off at the same coffee and donut shop I'd visited the day before. I got coffee and cigarettes and went to sit on the curb. What now? In a little while, there appeared the same young man I'd tried to help the day before, the guy who'd then robbed me.

"Got any change?"

Behaving like a prostitute with her pimp, I gave him my remaining money.

"This is all I've got, and I had to work for it. Do you know what I mean by 'work for it'?"

"Yes."

"Now I need you to take me to my car. I got lost last night trying to find it."

He pocketed the money and ran off, calling over his shoulder the address of the house.

Once again, I tromped through the neighborhood, getting more and more lost and forgetting the address. I went in ever widening circles and ended up in a completely different area of town. It was cold, and I didn't know what else to do but walk.

When night came, I was downtown and realized I'd need to find a place to sleep. I finally found an alleyway, wrapped myself tighter in my jacket, and lay down in the filth. From time to time I called out my demands to the world at large: "Bring me a carton of cigarettes and a gallon of brandy!" I waited in vain for my demands to be met. Once a person came down the alley and peered at me. I shot upright.

"What do you want?" I growled, trying to be threatening.

"Just checking to see if you were dead."

It was too cold to lie there. I got up and began walking again. I found myself in a deserted industrial district, very tired but needing to walk to stay warm. "This is my dark night of the soul," I decided. As I walked past trucks, buildings, discarded tires, I contemplated Christ. Would he save me? Had his sacrifice worked? The longer I walked, the colder it got, the more tired I became. I came to the bleak decision that his sacrifice had been for nothing. Then a ray of hope shot through me: "Still, it was not in vain. It was worth doing."

In this deserted area, a car came by and slowed.

"Get in," called the driver. "I'll give you twenty dollars."

"Not interested."

"I'll give you forty dollars."

"Go away."

He finally took off and accelerated into the night.

The next morning I discovered a piece of costume jewelry in my pocket and tried to trade it for a cup of coffee, but I found no takers. I kept walking. After a while, I found I was approaching a hospital. "I have the power to heal these people and spring them," I decided. Carefully, I paced around the building and sang a song of healing, confident that my movements were working miracles.

Later that day, I found myself circling a jail. Here again, I knew I had the power to set all the inmates free. Again I paced, slowly and deliberately, singing, "When the walls come tumbling down." Maybe not at once, but certainly in the future, the walls would tumble and the cell doors would fling open wide. Did not the Bible describe just such an event? And I, with my supernatural power, could make it happen again.

Night again. I was exhausted from my powerful day. Surely, I was through. It was time to be transported to Heaven and glory. I began to sing: "Swing low, sweet chariot, coming for to carry me home." Any time now, my chariot would come. Maybe by midnight. I fully expected to see it, lined with gold and surrounded by angels. I was ready. But it did not arrive.

Spotting an entrance to the subway, I went down the stairs and looked for a warm place to wait for my chariot. I curled up in the corner on the tile and was soon asleep, only to be wakened in what felt like moments later by a security guard.

"Sorry, but you can't sleep here. You'll have to move on."

Wearily, I climbed the stairs and kept going. Why had my chariot not come? All in God's time, not mine, I decided. I walked until I came to a big bank with a garden in front. I walked into it and lay down on the ground, so that I was covered by bushes. Soon enough, a bank security guard wakened me and told me I'd have to move on. As I rose, I saw a package placed where my head had been. It was a bag from MacDonald's, containing a hamburger and Coke. While I slept, someone had seen me and taken pity. I devoured the burger but discarded the Coke. It was too cold for an iced drink.

The next day, as I entered a park, I got a message to my brain that a false angel, a messenger from Satan, was challenging me to do battle. I was ready! I found a deserted place in the park and began to fight, swinging my arms and shouting out quotations from the Bible and the works of James Joyce and William Blake, visionaries I had studied years before.

It was a long battle, but I won. I turned, expecting crowds applauding, but no one in the park appeared to notice me. They were paying attention to a concert that was starting.

I walked along the outskirts, wondering if possibly tonight my chariot would come, when I spotted a couple of men drinking coffee.

"Could I get a sip?"

"Here, have the whole cup. You look like you can use it."

"Thank you, thank you."

I wandered off to enjoy my coffee and discovered that he had spiked it with whiskey. It tasted delicious and warmed me. Immediately, I wanted more, but my benefactor had gone. I resigned myself to another night pacing the streets and looking for a nook to sleep in.

Days passed, spent in aimless walking. Yet, I was still convinced that I had immense powers. As I passed different neighborhoods, I claimed them for countries I liked: this block for England, that one for France. Soon, I was sure, I would have my own large castle.

One day in the late afternoon, I realized that I was ravenously hungry. How long had it been since I'd eaten? Days, surely. I knew exactly what to do. I would find an unsuspecting victim, kill him, and eat his flesh. Survival of the fittest. About that time, a middle-aged black man came out of his shop.

"Good afternoon. What's going on?"

"I'm starving. I'm on the lookout for someone to kill and eat."

"Better come with me. I'll get you something to eat."

He drove me to a local place and ordered me a meatloaf plate to go. Then he drove to a ratty motel and got us a room. Once there, I devoured the food and announced that I needed a shower. When I was clean and dressed, I came out to find him under the covers watching television. He motioned for me to join him. To my disgust, he was naked under the sheets.

"Just kiss it," he said, pleading.

I was adamant. No sex in any form. I wasn't that kind of woman. When, oh when, would these men leave me alone? That time, I was fortunate. He left, and I got a night indoors.

A few days later, hungry and tired again, I walked through a neighborhood until I spotted a likely house and knocked on the front door. It was opened by an older man in casual clothes and slippers.

"I'm really hungry. Would you give me something to eat?"

"Of course. Come right in."

He fixed me a sandwich and offered a bath, which sounded good to me. I went upstairs and luxuriated in a hot bath and shampoo. Then I noticed to my horror that he had set something out for me to wear, clean clothes. It was a frilly pink dress, like a little girl's dress except larger.

Convinced he was a pederast who wanted me to pretend to be a little girl, I quickly dressed in my own clothes, slipped out the back door, and ran away.

Then came a moment of startling clarity. What was I doing here without money? After all, I still had an IRA account I could use. All

I had to do was call them, and I'd have lots of money at my disposal. Their phone number must be back at the condo with my records.

I walked until I found a group of taxis. I approached one after another, trying to get a ride back into South Pasadena. They all turned me down, but one finally said, "Do you have money for the fare?"

"Not on me, but I can get it once you drop me off. I'll even pay you double."

"Get in. The other guys told me not to take you, that you were a street person, but I'll take a chance. Consider it my good deed for the night."

Once we reached South Pasadena, I directed him first to my pastor's house. I rang the bell over and over, but no one answered. Enraged, I pulled potted plants from their pots. Next I directed him to the home of a man who had been a member of my church and was a one-time chief of police. Again, no answer. Again, I showed my displeasure by throwing decorations off his porch.

Next I directed him to the home of a man I'd known for ten years through a sobriety group. This time I rang and rang, knocked, and called his name over and over. No answer. He was hiding in there, afraid of me! I'd show him. With what seemed to me to be supernatural power, I pulled the license plate off his car and took it with me.

All right. I had no other choice. I directed the cab driver to my mother's condo. I rang the intercom and she answered.

"I need you to come down and pay off a cab."

"It's two in the morning."

"The cab is waiting."

Soon my mother emerged and wrote a check for the driver, exclaiming at the expense. Once I'd given him the check, I tore into her.

"This is the least you can do for me! You tricked me and tried to imprison me! You are my enemy!"

She ran back into the condo. I had the driver drop me off at the 24-hour coffee shop, where I hid the license plate in the planter box outside and managed to talk my way into a cup of coffee. There, I spent the rest of the night. From time to time, I'd go out to the patio and bum cigarettes off the smokers. I also performed a dance on the patio, using the squares in the cement to count off the Chain of Command.

At one point, I met up with a man I'd known years before. He told me his birthday was coming up, and I offered to throw a lavish dinner party for him. He was quite pleased. He told me he'd been out drinking that night and had got into it with someone at the bar. He'd escaped, but now the person was looking for him to beat him up. I immediately went back out to the patio, where I issued a mental challenge to the bully, telepathing him to meet me behind the bar for a wrestling match, which I was confident I could win.

The next morning, I was very weary and began to look for a place to sleep. In my wanderings, I found several large cardboard boxes in a Dumpster behind another café. I quickly made myself a nest and slept. I was awakened by two policemen, local cops.

"I'm sorry, ma'am, but we can't let you sleep here. The owner has complained."

"Where can I go?"

"Let us take you to Union Station, the local homeless shelter."

I got in the car with them and they transported me to the shelter. I was grumpy about being dumped there. After all, here was I, a woman with supernatural powers and two businesses to run, the theater and Heart. I also knew that the shelter catered primarily to homeless men. Nevertheless, I decided to make the best of it.

A twelve-step meeting was just beginning, and I entered the room. I was immediately disgusted by the leader, who was speaking on the importance of staying clean and sober and telling the crowd exactly how to do it. I began one of my rants.

"You know, gang, you don't have to listen to this garbage. No one has the right to tell you how to live your life. Don't let anyone dictate to you. Remember your human rights! Remember your freedom!"

The leader promptly asked me to leave the meeting. I did leave, continuing my speech as I exited. I made my way around to the back

DENISE B.

of the shelter, where I found a homeless man slouched against the wall, glumly studying his discharge papers from the hospital.

"What's wrong?"

"Got a broken arm."

"I can heal that. Let me see your papers."

He handed them over and I began to scribble all over them, convinced that my writing would indeed heal the arm. He became agitated.

"Give those back! I need them to get into the shelter!"

"I'm just trying to help you."

"You can help by making love to me. Healing love. Like Marvin Gaye."

I ran. Now what? I was in Pasadena now, close to trendy Old Town. Maybe if I went there, I could cadge a drink. I found a bar that faced Colorado Boulevard and took a stool. When the bartender came by, I ordered a shot of tequila, downed it, and quickly took off down the main drag.

I wandered into another bar, but I didn't find anyone willing to buy me a drink. A comedian was starting his show on a stage at the rear of the bar, and he asked for volunteers from the audience. I went up onstage.

"I'm Dr. Dee, a theatrical producer. Watch for my new play *Wheels*, which will be coming to a location near you soon." He quickly hustled me off stage.

Growing weary, I found yet another bar with a pool room that was not in use. I curled up on the carpet beneath a pool table and was able to sleep there for awhile. Once rousted, I went back out to Colorado Boulevard to panhandle, but was chased off by another bum whose street corner I was sitting on.

I remembered that I'd planned to use my IRA to set myself up in business, and I figured that my pastor would help me do it. I was a long way from the church, but I could make it, and in the morning I'd ask for his help. I walked and walked, humming and singing, eventually passing by ritzy houses where, I decided, I would go to ask for donations to Heart some day soon.

WIDE OPEN

Finally, I made it to the back of the church. There was chair out back, and I tried to cuddle up in it, but it was just too cold to get comfortable. How about starting a fire? A nice, safe fire. Wasn't fire the symbol of the Holy Spirit? Yes, of course. I prayed that whatever was not of God would be destroyed in the fire, and that everything that was of God would survive. There. Couldn't be safer than that.

I hauled a large metal trash can and began to fill it with combustibles: palm fronds from the lawn, paper and books that I'd left there after the play. I had matches in my pocket, and jubilantly lit the fire. Whoomph! There it was, blazing mightily. I warmed myself and then walked away, looking for a place to meditate.

I had no sooner settled myself on the lawn of the coffee shop when I was approached by two policemen. This time, they were not so sympathetic.

"Ma'am, we have witnesses who said you started a fire. You'll have to come with us."

Meekly, I let them cuff me and take me in to the station. There, I was questioned.

"Tell us what happened, ma'am."

"Well, I was going by my church when I heard a sound like vandals were coming, so I stayed out back for a while to protect the church. After that, deciding I had scared them off, I went to the coffee shop where you found me."

"Mm hmm. Wait here."

My story sounded plausible to me, but they were not buying it. Soon they transported me to the county jail, where they listed me as a person "dangerous to self or others," and from there to a mental hospital where I was booked in.

At the mental hospital, I was blind with rage. I had been trapped again! The staff gave me question after question in an intake interview, and then a psychiatrist took me to the back where there were many beds.

"This one will be yours. Look here. See how these curtains pull closed all around the bed? You can pull them and have all the privacy you need."

DENISE B.

He made it sound like a big privilege. I was suddenly too tired to care. I undressed, put on the nightgown they provided, and went to sleep.

PART TWO

Recovery

Chapter Three

When I awoke, I discovered that my shoes were gone and that my partial denture was gone, which gave me a gap-toothed grin. Not that I had anything to grin about. Had someone stolen my shoes? Had someone (hard to believe) stolen my denture? Or had I taken it out and lost it along the way?

I reported the loss. The person at the front desk commiserated and said she would report it. There was nothing else to do. Dinner came. I noticed that the other patients went out to a dining room, whereas I stayed in the day room. Why the inequity?

"You're on a 24-hour suicide watch. Nothing to worry about. Tomorrow you should be able to join the others."

After dinner came a smoke break. That was a relief. At the hospital, I learned, patients got three smoke breaks a day, one after each meal. It was cold out there on the patio, but I managed to trade a skirt I was wearing over my jeans for a few cigarettes. We were not allowed matches or lighters; a guard lit our smokes for us.

Then came medications. At first, I refused to take mine, but the orderly warned me that if I refused, I would only prolong my hospital stay, so I relented. I'd been put on a medication that was new to me: lithium. What was it for? Treatment of bipolar disorder, also known as manic depression. Still unwilling to concede that I was ill, I nevertheless took my medicine so I could be a cooperative patient and soon escape.

DENISE B.

The next day was blurry. I felt disoriented and strange. There were many interviews, with my doctor and staff members. One woman introduced herself as the activities director and expressed the hope that I would soon join her and other patients in games.

"I hope we will become friends and have some fun together while you are here."

"As long as you are part of the team that is keeping me locked up here, you are my enemy, not my friend."

As the day wore on, I felt an increasing panic. What was happening with my car? Was it lost to me forever? What was happening with my book publisher? I had to let her know that I was still interested, but how to explain I was in a mental institution? I tried desperately to get a staff member interested in my dilemma. I found one who would listen. She took some notes but made no promises.

That night, late, I awoke with a jolt. I and my fellow inmates, I realized, needed divine intervention. Specifically, we needed divine cleansing. Was I not an agent of God? I would provide it. I crept into the bathroom, where the lights were always on, and contemplated how best to achieve cleansing. How about a mighty gush of water? How delightful that would be. With a tremendous effort, I managed to wrench the sink fixtures out. Water indeed began to gush. Pleased, I scurried back to bed.

Very soon, I was roused by two irate staff members.

"The bathroom sink is broken, and it's a huge mess in there. We know you did it, so don't bother to deny it. Come with us right now."

They took me into an isolated unit and strapped me down on a narrow mattress on the floor. My thoughts began to race. Wasn't I scheduled to have a hearing in the morning to determine whether or not I could be released? How could I argue my case if I was strapped down? If I did have my hearing, what could I say to convince the judge? Would I be persuasive?

Finally, morning came. I was released only to be handcuffed with wrist and ankle cuffs. I was dismayed. This was hardly the way to make a good first impression. I was escorted to the hearing chamber and given a chance to talk. I spoke haltingly, trying to paint a picture of myself as a professional woman. I described my education, my teaching, my creative work, my new ministry to the homeless.

Then it was my doctor's turn to talk. Fluently, she described me as psychotic and extremely delusional. Among her examples was that I thought I was CEO of a corporation called Heart and that I believed a book of mine was about to be published. I tried to explain that Heart was simply a ministry of one, and that the book offer was real, but I'd had my turn. It was decided that I would not be released, but would stay until the doctor determined that I was no longer a threat to myself and others.

Glumly, I returned to the day room and began to survey my fellow inmates. They were a widely varied group, but all had two things in common: they all believed they were locked up through a tragic mistake, and they all wanted out. There was one woman who made a real pest of herself by pacing the bedroom area and declaiming loudly on the topic, how do you know if you are male or female? There was a very stout, dark-haired woman who rarely spoke. When I questioned her, she finally managed to mutter that her husband had put her in there, and all she wanted was to go home.

There was a pretty young woman who wept that she missed her two young children, that she believed her husband was abusing them, and that she was in here through some dreadful misunderstanding. There was a frightening large man who rarely spoke and who would not eat the hospital food. His wife came and brought him specially prepared food from home. He refused to bathe as well, so it was unpleasant to be in his presence. When I did try to start a conversation, he roared "Go away!" so I scuttled off.

There was a man about my age who explained that he'd been fired from his job and then evicted from his apartment. He moved to a motel and finally, overcome with the injustice of his situation, stood out on the motel lawn and began to give loud, angry speeches to passersby on how much a cruelly mistreated victim he was. The police were called, and they took him to the mental hospital, where he'd been before. After a few conversations, he asked me to marry him.

DENISE B.

"As soon as my mother dies, we'll have a house and money. You'll tolerate my homosexual affairs and we can start a church together, stressing the total forgiveness of God."

I told him I was flattered and would think it over.

As the days passed, I continued to try to get someone interested in my car and my book, but there was a large turnover in the staff and I'd no sooner ask one person then she'd be transferred and I'd have to start all over again.

Then, to my amazement, my pastor walked in. I was overjoyed to see him, and we hugged. We prayed together and then he asked what he could do to help. Relieved, I told him my worries about the car and the book, and he promised to do what he could and to visit regularly. I asked him please to bring me a cold soda and some cigarettes.

My next visitor was my daughter. I was very excited. Could it be that she had forgiven me my harsh words? She was very gentle and kind, and she assured me I would not be locked up forever. I asked her to bring me writing pads on her next visit.

Being on lithium, I discovered, meant I had to have frequent blood tests to determine whether or not I had the correct level in my system. The man who took my blood was inexperienced, and the needle hurt. However, I liked his friendliness. I dubbed him Dracula.

One Saturday morning we were given the opportunity to go to a 12-step panel that had come to visit. I elected to go, primarily to get out of the day room but also because I figured I had a lot to say about human rights and the unfairness of being locked up. I also hoped there would be coffee. At the hospital, we were only allowed decaf at meals.

The leader of the panel dashed my plans with his opening words.

"This is not a discussion meeting. You will listen, not talk. You will not get a chance to talk because you don't have anything we want. All you know is how to get yourselves locked up. We know how to get free."

Somewhat huffily, I listened. I'd brought a writing pad with me and began to draw caricatures of the people as they spoke. They took turns, each giving a brief version of his story before and after recovery from alcoholism. The stories were different but the message was the same: surrender to God, regain sanity, examine oneself, confess, make restitution, go frequently to meetings, pray and meditate, help others in need. It all sounded familiar from a lifetime ago. I realized that, if I ever got free, I'd have to start all over again. It was overwhelming.

Back in the day room, I found a copy of the book, *Alcoholics Anonymous*. Now I could express my own views without some stuck-up leader dictating to me. Leafing through the book, I found many flaws, repetitions, boring sections. I decided I would edit the book and, when I got out, start my own group with a new, improved book. I began ripping out pages that did not appeal to me, scribbling in the margins, changing words. "God" and "person" were no longer "he" but "she."

This editing was so much fun that I decided to do it with other books. I spent the afternoon ripping out pages and scribbling in margins. Immensely satisfying. Several times, I'd look out at the orderlies to see if they were coming to stop me. But they were busy with other tasks and ignored me. I decided that, as long as we were busy and happy, the staff left the inmates alone.

One night in the patio for a smoke break I befriended a new fellow from the other building who said he was a poet/songwriter but had no paper. I rushed in and got one of my pads for him. He was most grateful. He said he would only be at the hospital for a brief while. He'd been living on the streets in Hollywood and had gotten too cold and hungry. So he'd gone to a police station and told them he was ready to commit suicide. They deemed him a "danger to self" and took him in. He told me he did this from time to time when street life proved too hard. He'd sleep in a bed, eat three meals a day, get warm and healthy again, and then go back out.

For a week, we'd meet every evening and read each other our writings. His were mainly laments on unrequited love. Mine were mostly paeans to spiritual fire and water, my twin obsessions. Privately, I thought his work was sophomoric, and God only knows what he thought of mine, but to each other we were very supportive, full of praise. Our get-togethers were the highlight of my day.

Then one night I went out to the patio and he was gone. I was heartbroken. Why hadn't he even said goodbye? The call of the streets got too alluring, I guessed.

One day my pastor came with, he said, good and bad news. The good news was that my car had been found. It had been stolen and then abandoned; then it had accumulated many parking tickets and been towed. He'd been able to locate it through the tickets. He was willing to go, get it out of impound, and take it to a friend of his who was a mechanic. I was delighted and grateful.

Then came the bad news. He'd been in touch with my publisher, who was no longer willing to publish my book. She'd said that it sounded like I was close to being homeless myself, and that with my mental instability I would be too weak to embark on the public relations campaign she'd had in mind. My doctor had called her too, to assure her that my illness was very treatable and that I would soon recover, but she was adamant.

Well, it was very bad news. But if I had a strong reaction—breaking down, weeping—my doctor might decide I was still too unstable to be released. I went deep inside myself for strength and said, calmly, "That's a shame and a disappointment. However, the next step is clear. I'll rewrite it to emphasize the spiritual aspects and submit it to Christian publishers." Both the pastor and my doctor were impressed with my maturity, so I knew I'd made the right decision.

It was nearly Christmas. My daughter came with gifts: a couple of books and a pair of new shoes and a box of candy from my mother. I was very pleased and touched. Then my doctor said she'd like to speak with both of us privately, and we went to a room off the main hall.

She explained that while I was making progress, I was still ill and that she could not yet recommend release. I lost it completely, swearing at her and my daughter, accusing them of ganging up on me.

Then the horror of what I was doing came to me. How dare I lash out at my daughter when she had been so kind? What good was it to curse the doctor who was working to get me well? I bowed my head and apologized and pleaded for forgiveness.

Christmas itself was very bleak. There were no visitors. I huddled on the couch by the Christmas tree and held one of my new books in my hands, planning to edit it by ripping and scribbling. To my surprise, I found I'd lost my taste for destruction.

One day my doctor motioned me outside.

"Let's talk out here, where you can smoke if you want."

I was very grateful.

"I'd like to know what your goals are."

"My first goal is to get well and get out of here. Then I'd like to get my book published. Then I'd like to return to teaching. What are your goals?"

"My primary goal is to help people get well. My deepest wish is that each patient discover the healing power of Jesus Christ."

I was astounded. She'd never spoken of her faith before. Here I'd been thinking of her as my enemy, and we were actually on the same side. That moment became a turning point for me. I began to feel a kinship for my doctor and to believe that she wanted what was best for me.

That day, she loaned me a classic book on manic depression (bipolar disorder): *An Unquiet Mind* by Dr. Kay Jamison. As I read it, I was amazed by how it resonated. The author described the symptoms of her own mania: bursts of euphoria, surges of intense energy, increased creative powers, little need for sleep or food, highly inflated sense of one's own importance, periods of irrational rage, tendency to alienate those closest to one, to push them away. She might have been painting a picture of my own disease.

She then went on to describe the manic spending sprees, which often led to financial ruin. There too, I recognized myself: the belief that my supply of money was inexhaustible.

Once I'd read the book, I felt a profound relief. I had an illness. People understood it. It was treatable. I was not, at root, evil or bad. I could get well again. Like the author, I could go on to lead a productive life.

DENISE B.

The inmate who'd proposed to me made no further mention of marriage, but he did come up with a useful suggestion: we could both apply for disability insurance while we recovered. A friend of his got the paperwork for both of us. Very carefully, I filled it out, and my doctor was happy to fill in the doctor's section and sign off on it. The doctor assured me it would go through and recommended I be covered for a year.

At my request, my pastor brought several copies of the Bible in paperback, and I started up a Bible study among the inmates. We focused on the book of Luke, which I believed did a nice, clear job of setting forth the gospel.

Then I got the good news: I was ready to be released. However, I would have to go to a recovery home for a month, some place where the staff would administer my medication. A friend suggested Casa de las Amigas, a small home for women located in Pasadena. I called and was put on a waiting list for a bed.

When a spot opened, it was my birthday, January 16. I'd been in the hospital a month and a half. The doctor signed me out, the staff hugged me and bade me farewell and good luck, and I took off in a hospital van to my new home. It was the best birthday present I could imagine.

Once at Casa, I got processed in and resigned myself to a stay at another facility. I was surprised and delighted when an old friend came bustling in. She'd gotten special clearance to visit me. She brought me a warm sweater, toothpaste and toothbrush, socks, new tennis shoes, and other items. She gave me a big hug and assured me it wouldn't be too long before I was out and about again.

At Casa, the other women were friendly to me. We slept four or more to a room. Days were structured. We were awakened at six and we went immediately into morning chores, which varied week to week. Then we teamed up in groups of two or three and took a long morning walk, circling the block over and over. Then came breakfast. After breakfast there would be a meeting and then free time until lunch, where we could visit, smoke, shower, relax. After lunch came varying activities: a shopping trip once a week, a visit from a yoga instructor or other professionals, an interview with a counselor, etc. In the evening came dinner and then a drive in the Casa van to a different 12-step meeting each night. It was rigorous, and I began counting the days until I could be released.

One afternoon as I was relaxing with a soda I heard an inner voice speaking loud and clear: "You only took a few drinks while you were out there manic. No one knows about it. Why lose your sobriety over an understandable lapse? Just don't mention it to anyone and claim your eleven years as if nothing happened."

The voice of God? At first I believed it. Then, leafing through the *Big Book of Alcoholics Anonymous*, I reread the section on "rigorous honesty."

"There are those…who suffer from grave emotional and mental disorders, but many of them do recover if they have the capacity to be honest." (58) All right, there was my answer. I'd have to confess a relapse and begin again to build up sober years.

One evening the Casa group had been driven to a large Friday night meeting where I saw the man whose house I'd visited when I was looking for someone to pay my cab fare. When he hadn't answered my knock, I'd ripped his car license plate off in a fury. He spotted me, too, and to my amazement beamed at me and held his arms open wide for a hug. He was not upset over the license plate. He was relieved to see that I'd returned to the fold.

Visiting hours at Casa were very restricted. Family could come for a mixed meeting and then visit for an hour on Sunday only. This was a lonely day, as I had no visitors. However, amazingly enough, I got special permission to meet with my pastor during the week. He'd come during free time and help me get my life back in order. We discovered, to my profound relief, that I had not managed to break into my IRA during my manic spending spree. So I was able to make a withdrawal and pay for Casa, for the car's tune-up, for other expenses. He also took me to the DMV where I was able to get new photo ID and then to the bank, where I was able to close my old account and open a new one. When I explained that my checkbook had been stolen, the bank reimbursed me for the checks that the Los

Angeles thieves had written. Finally, he took me to a low cost eye clinic where I was able to get new glasses.

He remained in contact with my family and told me that my mother was happy about my recovery, forgave me, and wanted to help once I was released from Casa. The restraining order had expired, and she wanted me to come back home once I was released from the recovery center. I wept in gratitude.

Chapter Four

The day of my release finally came. Excitedly, I packed up my few belongings and sat in the lobby to await the arrival of a friend who was coming to pick me up. She was late, but she did come, and as I climbed into her car it was with a wonderful sense of release. Our first stop was the county hospital, where I would pick up medications for another month. She dropped me off and said she'd be back later that afternoon, that I was to wait in front.

The hospital was a maze, but I finally got registered, learned that from here on out I'd be getting services from a local clinic, and sat to wait for my medications. When my prescriptions were finally filled, I went back out to the front to wait again for my friend.

She drove me to my mother's place. My mother had prepared a welcome home dinner of roast chicken, mashed potatoes and beans. Shakily, I hugged her. I'd been uncertain of my welcome and apologized for my past behavior. Mom shrugged it off, saying, "Never mind. That was not the real you."

When the disability income came through, I was able to pay rent and begin to put my life back together again. I went back to church and to meetings, where again I was warmly welcomed. After a month, I went up to the local clinic and met with my new doctor.

"It's now been two months since I had a blood test, and I know that with lithium, regular blood tests are necessary."

"We won't need to do a blood test. The correct level was established at the hospital. All I have to do is make sure you keep steady at that same level."

DENISE B.

I thought his answer was odd, especially since I'd read in Jamison's book about the crucial necessity of frequent blood tests, but after all I loathed blood tests and he was the doctor. I accepted his judgment.

Come early summer, I decided on a way to make amends to my sister, who lived in San Jose. Her daughter was to perform in a play. I could fly up there, join the family in the audience, and then visit with my father and stepmother for a few days. My sister approved the plan, and I was off.

Once in San Jose, I got a chance to talk with my sister alone. She told me I was acting spaced out and strange. What should she do if I had a relapse? I didn't think anything was wrong, but I respected her fears and told her she should send me back to the hospital if I relapsed.

My niece did a good job in the play and I enjoyed it very much. However, at the celebration dinner afterward, I found I could not eat. Any kind of food, especially bread, made me nauseated. Maybe I had the 24-hour flu?

My father and stepmother, who'd also come for the performance, drove me farther north to their home in San Rafael. I was happy to spend time with them but my symptoms worsened. I was increasingly shaky and wobbly, and I still could not manage food. On the morning of my second day, my father announced that he was taking me to the hospital.

At the hospital, the doctors quickly determined that I had overdosed on lithium. I had dangerously high levels in my system. Saying that I was hours away from a coma, they put me on dialysis and a temporary pacemaker and an IV to flush the drug from my system. They took me off my other drug, Zyprexa, as well, just to be safe.

Without the Zyprexa, I began to hallucinate fiercely. The first night I was out cold, but the second night I became convinced that there was a murder plot to kill the head nurse and that only I could save her by solving the mystery. I didn't tell the doctors what was happening because to me, it seemed that my hallucinations were real, not fantasy. I was very relieved when the nurse I'd thought was a murder victim came to take my vital signs in the morning.

After a few days, the hallucinations faded and I was cleared to go home. My discharge papers, under "Instructions," said "Change doctors." My brother and his family also lived in Marin County, where the hospital was, so my sister-in-law picked me up to spend the day and night with them. I'd fly home in the morning. I was weak but pleased to have family time.

My little niece took me for a walk in the garden where, she told me, fairies lived in the hollyhocks. Could I see them? Oh, most definitely.

Upon returning home, I went back to the local clinic where I was placed on Depakote instead of lithium. This drug, my new doctor said, was not as high-maintenance and dangerous.

All went smoothly for a few days and then the hallucinations came back full force. Some were entertaining: at a meeting, I'd see little midget men dancing on the body of the speaker, singing a song. Some were terrifying: in the shower, I'd see the spray of water as composed of slivers of glass, coming out to cut me to shreds. When I sat down to read, knives would come shooting out of the book, aimed at my eyes.

In tears, I called my pastor and told him I could not bear it. He immediately went into action. He picked me up, took me back to the clinic, and demanded that we be seen by the new doctor immediately, no matter what his schedule was like. We did get in. The doctor was very soothing and said the hallucinations were easily gotten rid of by increasing my dose of Zyprexa. I was enormously relieved. The new dosage began to work very quickly, and soon I was free of the visual and auditory hallucinations.

Friends who heard of my hospitalization asked if I planned to file a malpractice suit against the doctor who had refused to monitor the lithium correctly. I did look into it, but I discovered that such a suit requires an initial large outlay of cash with no guarantee of winning. Still, what to do with the staggering hospital bills? My brother suggested I file for bankruptcy, and I looked into that too. After

DENISE B.

talking with a lawyer, I decided to go that route. It was straightforward, and before too long all my debt was wiped out. Fortunately, I filed before the new legislation requiring partial repayment took effect.

I resumed my life, content with church and AA, reading and visiting with friends, regular doctor visits. Once at a meeting I heard a speaker describe a year during which he'd had a nervous breakdown: severe depression and other symptoms.

"I knew that drugs were not the answer for me. The only thing to do was double up on my meetings and pray, and I did get through it."

I was aghast to imagine the unnecessary suffering that person had gone through because of a prejudice against medication. Yes, medication took a while to work and, as I had discovered, took a while to get the right dosage and type, but medication worked! Now that I was well again, I could not imagine life without it. I'd be back on the street, starving and crazed, belligerent and miserable. I could only hope that no one in the audience gave credence to the speaker. I believed that he could cause real damage with his message, and I became very annoyed with the school of thought that declares psychiatric medications violate sobriety. I decided, then and there, to be honest about my own story and try to counter that damage.

Late that summer, I got a phone call from Mission College. Could I please teach again in the fall? I was delighted and quickly accepted, filled with gratitude that they had disregarded my resignation letter, taken it as need for a break only, and given me another chance. So I began to work again, taking pleasure in it.

Today, life is good. I have a fine psychiatrist who monitors my medication closely. He has diagnosed me as a bipolar personality with schizo-affective disorder, which explains the symptoms. Both are highly treatable. My mind is clear and my emotions stable.

I have built up my teaching so that I now have four to five classes a semester at three different schools. I enjoy the eagerness and passion of my young students, and I love to visit with them before class to hear them speak of their hopes and dreams.

WIDE OPEN

My family and I get along well, and in June of 2006 I became a grandmother, which is a source of joy to me. I marvel at the new one, go to see her as often as possible, and am filled with gratitude that I get to be part of her life. My family has forgiven me the excesses of mania and welcomed me back into the fold. I go out with friends to eat and to movies. Life is once again calm, happy, and productive.

My psychiatrist, upon learning that I enjoy writing, recommended that I begin this project, saying, "You have a textbook case of manic depression. Why not write about it? You could help people by doing it." So I have, and it is my sincere hope that indeed, people will be helped by this document.

PART THREE

Steps to Murder
An AA Mystery

By Nancy D.

Foreword

The subtitle of this book promises "...and her return to sanity." Therefore, I have decided to include *Steps to Murder*, pen name "Nancy D.," a piece that was written in the summer of 2007, seven years after a combination of psychiatry, religion, and AA repaired my brokenness.

Many artists, writers, and musicians are and have been manic depressive. The tremendous upsurge of creativity that mania brings with it often produces highly original work. (In my case, it was the play *Wheels*.) It is also true that, for that very reason, people are reluctant to seek treatment. There is a fear that to lose the manic highs is also to lose the creative spirit.

I shared that fear. I suspected that while medication was able to give me a calm and orderly life, it would also rob me of the ability to write creatively. Sanity restored, would not things become disappointingly flat and dull?

I discovered that the creative impulse was not killed off by medication. It might hibernate for a while, but it was still there. So it was that I began to wonder if, given my love of mysteries, I might be able to write one myself. The following novella, *Steps to Murder*, is the result. It was tremendous fun to write.

Some of the characters in the novella are pure invention. Others, with changes, are drawn from life. Still, this remains a work of fiction, and all events are imaginary. The purpose is simply to entertain. The setting is the San Gabriel Valley, with an emphasis on South Pasadena, so there is local color.

Questions on police procedure were answered willingly by the South Pasadena Police Department and the Los Angeles County Sheriff's Department, and I was most impressed by their willingness to help.

Happy reading.

Chapter One

Emily awoke and checked the clock. 4:45 am. Well, no need to have set the alarm for 7:00 after all. Her inner clock was still running on a work schedule. As the summer progressed, no doubt she'd wake up later and later, but for now she had the gift of a couple of hours free before it was time to get ready for church. Plenty of time for devotions and possibly a letter or two.

She counted out her morning pills and took them to the dining room table, where she'd have juice and breakfast later. As she often did, she thanked God for these tablets that made it possible for her to lead a normal life despite her manic depression. What if she'd been born in an earlier era, before good medication had been discovered? What a nightmare; she'd be relegated to an asylum for sure. Locked up and forgotten. Or, like earlier artists, she might have committed suicide. Virgina Woolf came to mind. But today, as long as she took her meds, she was safe and secure.

First things first: she got the coffee going and took a cup out to the patio. Still dark out, but it felt like it was going to be a lovely day. None of the marine layer that the locals had dubbed "June gloom." She lit a cigarette to go with the coffee and began her morning prayers. The ritual was soothing.

"Dear God, I surrender to Thee. Please take me and make me into the person you would have me be. Please also remove my defects of character, especially worry and fear, and replace them with your Holy Spirit. Please may I have your blessing on this day ahead:

preparation time, stamina for church, pleasant afternoon and evening. Please solve my difficulties: may my classes fill for fall semester; may unemployment insurance come through for the summer; may retirement provide sufficient income when I'm ready for it."

There. That was the first round. Her prayers, she knew, reflected whatever her current worries were. Some would say that the only legitimate prayer, after surrender to God, was a simple request for "knowledge of his Will for us and the power to carry that out," in accordance with Step 11. But Emily could not resist bringing present concerns to the Throne. She figured it couldn't hurt to remind God what was on her mind. It helped to talk things out as she would to a friend. And what better friend could she have, after all?

Now, with still plenty of time before getting ready, how about a letter to her father. He was in a retirement community up in northern California, and he'd told her how much he looked forward to her letters. She moved into the living room, where her computer was set up, and entered the word processing program.

Dear Dad,

Summer beckons. I have only one more day of teaching to go. Monday I head out to Pasadena City College, where I'm hoping to meet with the students and also get their grades calculated and turned in all on the same day. Then I'll be free until fall!

All three of my schools have sent me a memo saying that part-time teachers qualify for unemployment insurance over the summer, since we are not salaried employees but contract labor. So I will, of course, apply. It will be nice to have a steady if modest income during the summer months.

I really enjoyed reading the final exam essays at Glendale Community College. I like teaching there. I think it's because the students get well trained in high school at Glendale and so are prepared for college when they come. I had them write an essay interpreting the ending of Viramontes' *Under the Feet of Jesus*. That's trickier than it sounds, because she has written an open ending: all the loose ends of plot are left untied, unlike a novel like one by Dickens, where everything is resolved at the end. They came up with some really creative solutions. Some created a happy ending for all concerned, while others got very existential and bleak.

They seemed to really enjoy the book, so I'm glad I chose it. You'd like it too, since you like Steinbeck. She writes about a family of migrant farm workers, very realistically, with vivid imagery. I highly recommend it.

One quirk of teaching: in the course of a fifteen week semester, I get really close to my students, interested in their hopes and dreams. Then, it's over and time to move on. They move forward with their lives and I with mine, until the next batch arrives with a new semester.

My plans for the summer are low-key. I do intend to make it to an AA meeting every day, which is something I haven't been able to do since I first got sober 18 years ago. What a luxury. Meetings keep me on an even keel and make me happy, and it will be great to re-connect with the people there whom I haven't seen in a while.

Of course I also want to just rest and relax and read lots of mysteries. Then I'd like to go out with friends for lunch and movies. What are your plans? Shall I come up for a visit? Let's work out a time that's good for both of us. I'd love to see you, and maybe we can take in some of the sights of San Francisco when I'm up.

How are you getting along? Do you like the new place? I'll bet the ladies are vying for your attention. Hope the food is good and that the Manor has some interesting field trips planned. Do you miss having a car? I thought I could either rent a car when I come up or drive up instead of fly, so we'll have wheels.

Well, it's time to get ready for church. I'll talk with you soon.

Love,
Emily

DENISE B.

Okay, her dad was updated. And she'd already emailed her mother, who'd moved with her stepfather to Santa Barbara, last night. Her mother had recently discovered email and loved it, using it frequently. She too had suggested a visit. It was fortunate that her parents had chosen such scenic places to live.

She took her time getting ready. Juice with pills, breakfast of English muffin and lemon curd, lovely hot shower and shampoo. What to wear? June was so tricky, cool in the morning and often hot in the afternoon. She decided on a light brown and coral outfit: brown corduroy pants, coral tee, light sweater patterned in both colors. It had been a Christmas gift from her mother and was very becoming. Emily, at 59, didn't mind her mother's dressing her. Oh, she once had—in college all "outfits" had been relegated to the back of the closet while she'd lived in jeans and t-shirts. But these days, she was happy to benefit from her mother's good fashion sense.

Makeup, then a second cup of coffee and a second round of prayers, this time for others. As she went down the list of others' needs, she was reminded again of the AA policy: only pray for God's will in the situation. Okay, so she added a coda: "may thy will be done in these as in all my prayers." Sometimes these prayers were answered quickly and sometimes it took quite a while. One name had been on the work list for almost a year now. Emily hoped the young man in question would find something soon. He was living with his mother and really needed to establish some independence.

Grace Church was only a short drive away. One of the best parts of living in South Pasadena, Emily had discovered, was that everything—church, post office, library, market—was minutes away. She was early enough to socialize and went over to give Jane Hendricks, the pastor's wife, a hug.

"Are you out of school yet, Jane?"

Jane taught third grade. She was a beautiful woman with dark glossy brown hair, sparkly blue eyes, and a sweet smile. Emily was sure she was popular with the children she taught. She was also reminded, each time she saw Jane, of the pastor's sermon on marriage. He'd claimed it was the husband's job to make sure that his wife felt loved and beautiful. Clearly, he practiced what he preached.

"One more week to go. We'll just be doing fun stuff, since it's too close to summer for them to really concentrate on something new. It'll be great to be able to work in the garden. Also, I want to get by the library to see if they've got the latest Cat Who mystery to start my summer reading."

"Yes, they've got it. It's in the rental section. I checked it out and enjoyed it very much."

"When we're both off, we should take walks together. I've been neglecting exercise. How about it?"

"Sounds like a good idea."

Emily moved to her usual spot up front and was dismayed to see a copy of *The Education Reporter*, an extremely right-wing newspaper, waiting for her. It was, she knew, a gift from Katharine, an older woman who was very conservative and wanted Emily to share her beliefs.

"I'm a Democrat, Katharine," she had said gently.

"But how can you be? They're wrong about everything!"

"Nevertheless."

Undeterred, Katharine had begun a conversion campaign, and this newspaper was one of her strategies. Emily leafed through it. There was an article on teaching abstinence in school instead of safe sex. There too was an article on the school shooting at Virginia Tech. The shooter, a young man who had killed many before turning his gun on himself, had been an English major. The writer linked his shooting spree with the fact that the English faculty was very liberal and offered courses with a feminist and Marxist slant. Could it be that their liberal views had tipped him over the edge? Disgusted, Emily set the newspaper down. She usually tossed it unread, and she wished she had done the same with this issue. It upset her.

The piano player began the prelude, so Emily tried to calm her thoughts. There was nothing she could do about Katharine's beliefs, so she'd need to pray for her simply that God would bless her. Nothing she could do? Maybe there was. Maybe she could be bold and tell the woman that she was offended by the newspaper so to please stop sharing it.

DENISE B.

She was pleased to note that today they'd be using the hymnals. Often music at church was led by a praise band, lyrics projected on the wall. That was fun but the more traditional hymns were her favorite. Today, she saw, they'd be singing "When I Survey the Wondrous Cross."

After a few hymns, it was time for prayer requests. One man was going in for cancer surgery. One woman had lost a brother and wanted help through her grief. A daughter was facing a difficult licensing exam and needed good focus and concentration. Emily made notes in the bulletin; she'd add the names to her morning prayers. It was this, being part of a family of believers who genuinely cared for and wanted to help each other, that had drawn her to the church in the first place.

Jane's husband Paul took his stand behind the pulpit. Now here was why Jane had prayed for stamina. Pastor Paul's carefully researched sermons usually lasted 35-40 minutes and required all her attention. Emily appreciated the research but knew she had to be really ready to focus, as she had in her school days.

This morning he gave a background on Jewish law in the time of Christ, to illustrate how badly Jesus was railroaded when he was taken to court. In condemning Jesus, the officials had blatantly disregarded the law. The gist: life is unfair, but nevertheless God is at work. He ended with the words of Christ, "In this world you will have tribulation. But be of good cheer: I have overcome the world." Emily felt her body and soul relax with the comfort of the words, which were in her personal list of all-time greats.

Leaving church, she stopped to speak with several people. One, to let him know she'd be praying for his cancer surgery. Two, to thank her again for a small dinner party. Three, to inquire if she'd learned how to ride her new motor scooter yet, so that she wouldn't have to walk such long distances. Grace Church was small and tightly knit; Emily knew that whatever came her way, she wouldn't have to face it alone.

Lunch was cottage cheese and fruit. It was still cool enough to eat outdoors so she did, on the look-out for hummingbirds who might be attracted by the bright red feeder her dad had sent. He was an avid birdwatcher. None came today, but maybe they'd show later in the week.

After lunch, she discovered that the article she'd read at church still rankled. Maybe if she wrote about it? Why not? She moved to the computer and began by first summarizing the article and giving her response to it.

"As an English teacher, I also teach the logical fallacies. I want the students to be able to recognize and avoid fallacious reasoning in their own work and the work of others. The article blaming Cho's killing spree on his liberal teachers exemplifies the fallacy known as false cause. Just because something happened before another thing in chronological time does not mean that the first (Cho's attending class) caused the second (Cho's rampage). This is irresponsible journalism.

"I considered saving the article and using it as an example of fallacious writing but ultimately decided to consign it, along with its brethren, to the circular file. Propaganda, coming from the right or the left, disturbs my peace of mind."

Saving the piece under "Fallacy," she reflected on the healing power of writing. Her resentment toward the original article was gone. She felt cleansed.

The rest of the afternoon was free and clear, so she picked up a new Spanish mystery by Rebeca Pawel, *The Summer Snow*. Soon she was immersed in post World War Two Spain. It was a period she was unfamiliar with, and she marveled at the author's careful scholarship. The jangling of the phone startled her.

"Hello?"

"Professor Davies? This is Armen from your English 101 at Glendale? I was wondering about my grade in the course."

Armen's young, flute-like voice full of tentative questions evoked his presence in the class. He was actually a high-school student on a fast track, taking a college course in preparation for his entry into a four-year university. His shyness in class was belied by his bravado in his papers, where he'd tested her with increasingly bold sexual innuendo. She understood his concern. She'd finally shut him down by giving him a D on the midterm, wherein he'd pictured liberals as huge walking penises. She'd asked the class to contrast liberals and conservatives, and most of the students had responded with thoughtful answers, but young Armen had wanted to see just how far he could go. "You're capable of strong writing," she'd commented in red, "but you need to take the exam question more seriously and not treat it as a spoof." He'd done much better on the final, tending toward the poetic.

"You got a B, Armen."

"Oh, a B. Okay. Thank you."

It was Emily's practice to give students her home telephone number on the syllabus each semester. Some of her friends questioned the policy, saying she'd be driven nuts by calls and excuses, but overall she enjoyed the accessibility it gave her to her students. Some teachers, she knew, used email, but that seemed like too much work to her. Undoubtedly there would be late papers mingled in with the SPAM, and frantic pleas she'd miss unless she checked email hourly.

Emily checked her wristwatch. Time had flown by. She was due at Marianne's in half an hour. She locked the door to the patio, packed cigarettes into her purse, and headed out the front door.

The drive to Marianne's took her through the curving, tree lined streets of San Marino and then up South Lake, Pasadena's main shopping street. Just off Lake she made a right and onto Marianne's street. Perfect: there was a parking space. She walked down the block to the townhouses and keyed #25 into the intercom.

"Hello?"

"Hi, Alex. It's Emily."

"Hey, Emily. Hold on. She says she'll meet you downstairs."

When Marianne appeared, Emily was glad she'd stayed in her church clothes. Always elegant, her best friend was wearing a cowl-necked pink sweater and perfectly tailored black slacks. Her shoulder-length blonde hair looked to have just been cut and styled; her nails were shaped and polished to match the sweater.

"Hi there. You look marvelous."

"Thanks. Cute sweater. Do you want me to drive?"

"If you wouldn't mind. You're so good at parallel parking, and I just can't seem to do it."

They were headed for Brits, a place with a pub on one side and a restaurant on the other. For their biweekly dinner dates, they took turns choosing the restaurant. Lately, Emily had gotten into the habit of choosing Brits.

Expertly, Marianne backed out of the parking garage and headed for Colorado Boulevard. She turned down the classic rock station on the car radio.

"So are you almost out of school?" she asked.

"Yes, thank God. Tomorrow is the last day. I don't go back until August 27."

"How I envy you. But you deserve it. I know how hard you work during the semester. I've got two weeks coming. Alex and I are thinking of going to New York."

"Sounds terrific. Maybe you can get in some good shows. How is Alex?"

Marianne laughed.

"Still avoiding meetings. He must think he can stay sober vicariously through me. Still, it's his choice. Nothing I can say will make a difference."

"Did you get to the War Memorial today?" The War Memorial meeting, named for the building that housed it, was held Sundays from 11:30 to 1:00. It was Marianne's favorite.

"Yes, I made it. The speaker was pretty good. He started drinking in Vietnam, right after high school. He had some interesting stories. He was about ten years sober."

"Oh yes, Vietnam. I was in high school when we went in. My first boyfriend was drafted. He made it through, but he was never the same. It changed him drastically."

"So the speaker said. Now that school's out and you don't have papers to grade, do you think you'll come back to that meeting?"

"Honestly, no. I'll be able to get to a meeting six days a week, but not Sundays. I've discovered that my attention span is too short. I can't both listen to a sermon at church and then go listen to a 40-minute speech. I'd be going nuts halfway through."

"I can see that. It's simpler for me, since AA is my church."

They arrived. As always, Emily marveled at Marianne's ability to slide the car right into a space. Once inside, Marianne greeted the owner, whom she knew. Since it was early, they had their choice of tables. A waiter soon appeared. Both knew what they wanted. For Emily, bangers and mash with extra gravy. For Marianne, fish and chips without the chips. Emily knew that her friend's self-restraint was the cause of her remaining so slender, but she herself could not resist the mashed potatoes and gravy. They went so well with the plump sausages.

"I tell you what. I can't make the War Memorial, but I've been thinking of going back to the big Friday night meeting. Do you still go to that one?"

"I do. That would be great. Want to meet me there?"

"Sure. 7:30. We used to call that one the Meat Market. Is it still?"

"Oh yeah, people still cruise. Lots of newcomers go there; the recovery houses drive them. And they're always on the make, ignoring their sponsors' advice to stay out of a relationship for the first year. Why do you ask? Want to start dating again?" Marianne teased.

"Heavens, no. I wouldn't know where to begin. I've been on my own for eighteen years now, as long as I've known you. No, the only guy who interests me is James, but he's made it clear he wants to remain just friends. I'd thought that since we were both teachers and liked crosswords that we might have enough common ground, but it seems like all he wants to do is go camping in the wilderness with his new dog."

"Yeah, he strikes me as too passive for you. Didn't he just get out of a relationship?"

"Yes, and he's gun shy now."

"Well, if it's meant to happen it will. Anyway, a relationship is not all it's cracked up to be. Alex only consults every now and then, so he's usually home. But he still expects me to work all day, then come home and make him dinner. Then on weekends I clean the place, and he doesn't lift a finger."

"That's archaic, Marianne."

"I know it. But if I don't do it, it won't get done."

Once they'd finished their meal, the women ambled up the block and across the street to Starbuck's. There, they used Emily's gift card from her stepsister to purchase drinks. Both smokers, they chose a table outdoors.

"How's work?" Marianne was a top echelon legal secretary with a firm in downtown Los Angeles.

"Pretty interesting, actually. We've had some good cases. And the lawyers treat me well."

"They should. You do really good work for them. When will you be able to retire?"

"The benefits package is decent. I expect around 65. How about you?"

"At least 70. I came to teaching late in life, and I'm not even vested yet since I work part-time. Also, the deal now is that if people draw teachers' retirement, they can only claim a small percentage of their social security."

"That's so unfair."

"I agree. Congress is considering a bill to repeal that law, but no action yet."

"What I think we should do, when we retire, is get a small group of women together. Share a big place, everyone helping with expenses, and look out for each other."

"Sounds good. Count me in."

Once they'd finished their coffees, Marianne dropped Emily off at her car. Looking forward to a few more chapters of the novel, Emily drove home. Pawel did not disappoint. Lots of detail on postwar Spain and good, interesting characters.

DENISE B.

Time to get ready for bed. Feeling very diligent, Emily brushed and flossed her teeth, washed and creamed her face. Might as well take care of the old body, since it was the only one she had. Last step: nighttime pills. More Depakote to keep her moods stabilized, and an additional Zyprexa to prevent the hallucinations that came from her schizoid tendencies. With a shudder, Emily recalled what it had been like when the hallucinations started: waking in the middle of the night, hearing loud voices outside the window mocking her. Knowing they weren't real but being unable to move for fear of them. It had been debilitating, and then it had been such a relief to tell her psychiatrist and get his response: "That problem is very easily solved."

Emily knew there was a school of AA thought that believed and preached that psychiatric medications should not be taken as they broke a person's sobriety. Indignantly, she wondered how many people were silently suffering needless mental anguish out of fear that to get help spelled an end to their sobriety. Of course, she herself had been initially reluctant to take the meds. Her first reaction when the psychiatrist had told her she'd need to be on medication for the rest of her life had been disbelief. Fortunately for her, he'd been very savvy.

"If you don't believe me, ask your AA sponsor," he'd counseled. She had. And her sponsor, who herself had suffered depression off and on, insisted she go on the medication at once.

After thanking God for another sober day, Emily climbed into bed. Relaxing, she began a mini-inventory. What had gone right? She'd connected with her father, with Jane, with Marianne. She'd been firm with Armen. She'd given herself fun time with writing and reading.

What had gone wrong? She'd forgotten to thank Pastor Paul for his sermon. How could she remedy that? Zap him a quick email tomorrow. She'd allowed herself to get very upset by Katharine's newspaper and hadn't said a word. Solution? Speak with the woman, being polite but firm. Ask her to stop passing the newspaper along.

Any other amends to make? She couldn't think of any. All in all, an excellent day. Emily drifted off to sleep with a smile on her face.

Chapter Two

Monday morning at 9:00, Emily set off for the 10:30 Women's Step Study meeting. She was coffee maker, and she liked to have everything ready by the time people began arriving. She took Orange Grove all the way, admiring the Tournament House as she passed it. Once, when she'd gone to the New Year's Day Rose Parade, she'd been outside the large white mansion when the royal court was leaving it to get on their float. How lovely and excited they had been. As a teenager, she'd wanted to be a beauty queen but had never made the semi-finals. She'd figured that her hair was too curly and unruly, her lips, although cupid-bow, too narrow. Both legacies from her grandmother. Since her grandmother had also left her enough money to buy a car, she once again offered silent thanks.

She made a left just above Walnut and into the parking lot of Neighborhood Church. Normally she'd take her copy of *Twelve Steps and Twelve Traditions*, the meeting's text, but today she wouldn't be able to stay for the book study, just the leader's story. As she walked through the beautiful, tree-lined grounds, she thought she should really take the stairs if she wanted to lose ten pounds, but her instinct led her to the elevator.

She was pleased to see that the church custodian had preceded her. Chairs were set out in neat rows, tables were erected, and two large coffee pots were plugged in. One, for hot water, was already squealing and moaning, indicating that it was almost done. She scooped coffee into the second, following the method she'd been taught in her early days of sobriety: one Styrofoam cup of coffee for every ten cups of water. Flipping the switch to "on," she stood with her ear pressed against the pot, waiting to hear the starting perk. Nothing happened, but she did notice that the outside of the pot was already hot. She went to the sink and tested the water: it came out hot. Rule two of coffee making was to always start with cold water.

She walked downstairs to hunt for the custodian. She found him in his office, strapping tools to his belt.

"Jaime, the coffeepot isn't working. It needs to be filled with cold water."

"Okay. I'll be right there."

This time, not wanting to appear lazy, she took the stairs with Jaime following. He too tested the faucet and was surprised that the water flowed very hot.

"Easy to fix. I'll just let it run until it runs cold again." Now why hadn't she thought of that? Soon the problem was solved and the coffee was perking away.

Emily set out cups, stirrers, sugar and creamer, tea, instant decaf, napkins. And the job was done. Soon after, Irene arrived. Since she took an early bus, she was always the first to arrive. She plunked down her needlepoint and gave Emily a hug. Irene was solidly built, and the hug was heartening. A former beautician, she could when she chose look very glamorous, but today she was going casual and wore no makeup. Still, her inner beauty and goodness shone through.

"Would you pray with me this morning?" Irene and Emily were prayer partners, a practice that had developed through the years.

"Of course. What's up?"

"It's a woman who used to live in our apartment building with her teenage daughter. Last weekend they moved out and she said she was putting everything into storage. I haven't seen her, but Doug has, and he says they both seem to be living out of her car. Seeing as how you were homeless once, I thought of you right away. Is there anything you'd like to pray about?"

"Yes. Today I turn in the grades at Pasadena City College. As usual, I'd like to be both fair and accurate in assessing their work."

DENISE B.

They joined hands, and Emily began. "Dear Lord, we lift up to you this woman and her daughter who have joined the ranks of the homeless. We beg of you to intervene. Let them find and be willing to accept help. Bring them shelter, showers, enough to eat. Help the mother to find work so that she can support them once again. Thank you for putting them on Irene's heart."

Irene took over. "Dear Jesus, I second Emily's prayer. I also ask that you guide and direct her this day as she grades her students. Let her be neither too hard nor too easy. Let the students receive the grade they truly deserve. Thank you for giving her this teaching job. Amen."

They grinned at each other. Once again, they'd managed to sneak in prayer time before anyone else arrived. They thought of it as their secret, and they relied on it. Emily knew she'd miss Irene's company come fall semester, when her schedule changed and she'd have to miss the meeting.

"So, Emily. How about you? Are you still a bachelorette?"

What was with this? First Marianne and now Irene.

"Well you know, I've never had any luck with men. It's just not my strong suit. When I was drinking I was attracted to increasingly violent guys. When I first got sober, those experiences kept me away from men altogether. I was terrified of them. Then my sponsor suggested I stay away from relationships for the first year and get to know God better, so I got out of the habit of looking at men as potential sex partners, which was good. Now that I'm ready to trust again, there's really no one in the picture."

"Well, maybe you'll be like one of those singles described in the book. The kind who, freed from marriage, is able to render 'prodigies of service.'"

"There's always that. And how's it going with your search for a new sponsor?" Irene's long-term sponsor had died a few months earlier.

"I've been thinking about Sophie. I like what she has to say at the Wednesday Women's Group. And she's kind of like an elder stateswoman. What do you think?"

"Sophie's a good woman and very kind. I know she's helped a lot of people. I could never have her as a sponsor though, because she is against any kind of psychiatric medication. She believes that to take it is to break one's sobriety. And I feel very strongly about that. You know I have taken it for years. And without it, my sobriety would not be worth living: strange voices and hallucinations coming from every direction. Might as well get drunk and try to quell them that way."

"I see what you mean."

Emily marveled at the synchronicity of things. Here she'd been musing just last night on Sophie's school of thought, and now this morning Irene's question had given her a chance to articulate her views. It was an indication, she thought, that she was on the right track.

They heard voices on the stairs, and soon the room began to fill. The secretary, prompt as always, started by ringing her bell right at 10:30, and she passed the meeting over to the young woman she had asked to lead. The leader, Joy, had started drinking when she was only twelve. A chronic runaway, a ward of the court, experiences with many foster homes, she finally met a foster mother who was in AA and who was able to help her get sober at 20. Now she was 35, an interior decorator, happily married with twin sons. Pleased for Joy and also pleased that she'd managed to finish her story by 11:00, Emily slipped away to head for Pasadena City College.

Once on campus, she first stopped off at the café for a BLT on white toast. She was happy to find a table in the shade. The sandwich was delicious: crispy bacon, sweet tomato, crunchy lettuce.

Then she headed for the part-timers' computer lab to check her email, amazed as always by the amount of SPAM that accumulated overnight. How could there be so many offers for penis enlargement and online pharmacies, and how could the latter stay in business? Who would give out a credit card number to an unknown company? Weird.

There was one email from her mother: "Good luck on your last day! Still foggy here. Will let you know when the beaches are sunny

DENISE B.

so you can come up for the weekend." She replied with a thanks. It would be fun to make the trip up to Santa Barbara.

In the English department, she was pleased to find in her mailbox the scantron sheet for grades and the print-out from the Writing Lab telling her how many hours her students had logged in. With still time to spare, she headed for the drinks kiosk for a diet soda and sipped it while she smoked several cigarettes. Ruefully, she recalled how she and Marianne had requested prayer from Grace Church's Wednesday night prayer group for help in quitting smoking. That had been how many years ago now? And here they both still were, unrepentedly enjoying it. Ah, well.

As she relaxed before class, she eavesdropped on students gathered on the benches under a huge tree. One young man was boasting that he always cheated on his exams. He paid someone to take them for him. Emily hoped he'd get caught. One young lady told a friend how she'd worked on a final paper all weekend, how her printer had acted up, and how finally she'd had to take a cab to make it for her early morning final because she'd missed the bus. So such mishaps really did occur. When her students came up with similar stories, they were not necessarily just making up excuses.

Okay, time for the last class of the semester. Since the English department did not require her to give a final exam, she used the time to check everyone's journal and double check time spent in the Writing Lab. She was pleased that all but one student showed up.

Having assessed everyone's work, she dismissed the class and began calculating grades. She found herself rooting for her students to make it, and she was heartened to find that she could give five A's, only one D, and the rest B's and C's. Reminding herself that if she passed the D student, she wouldn't be doing him a favor, since he'd flounder in his next class, she went to photocopy her records, turn in one copy to the department, and finally turn in the original set to the Records office.

Then, hardly daring to believe that she was free for the summer, she headed home. Her cottage on Park Street was welcoming. Her cleaning lady, whom she'd found in AA, had been there in her absence, and the place gleamed.

Too early for dinner? Not really. She popped a frozen spaghetti dinner into the microwave, mixed a small salad, and ate while she finished up Pawel's novel. In the course of the book, she'd learned a lot of Spanish history. She'd also enjoyed the book's philosophical bent. Pawel, she discovered, taught high school while working on her series. Amazing. Did the woman never sleep?

Could she too write a mystery over the summer? Might be fun to try. She'd thought of a pastor keeling over after taking a sip of poisoned Communion wine but then had read something similar in a Jane Haddam novel. Besides, Pastor Hendricks might read it and think she wanted to kill him off. Give it an academic setting and have the killer pick off members of the English department? Possible, but there again she'd read several mysteries with a scholarly setting. Well, maybe something would come to her. She'd discuss it with Marianne.

Commonplaces to avoid: plucky protagonist in constant conflict with a cop who warns her repeatedly not to interfere in a police investigation; foolish protagonist who confronts the killer alone; heroine who takes it upon herself to solve the crime because she or a close friend has been falsely accused; clever protagonist who is in sharp contrast with bumbling, foolish cops; villain who heads a fanatical Christian cult. Those were all mystery elements that annoyed her.

Oh well. At least she knew what not to do. Maybe tomorrow she'd make some notes. In the meantime, she wanted to immerse herself in truly beautiful writing, so she went to the bookshelf and selected one of her favorites by Elizabeth George: *Deception on His Mind* .

To Emily, George represented writing at its purest. The author was bold in her characterization, never afraid to take side tracks if it gave her a chance to explore a character's personality quirks. She'd once written George a fan letter and had been delighted when, later, a postcard came in return.

She read until bedtime and did another mini-inventory. There didn't seem to be anything she'd need to make an amends for. She'd expressed her reservations about Sophie to Irene, but she'd also praised the woman. It didn't count as gossip. So it looked like she could sleep with a clear conscience.

The week flew by as Emily plunged back into daytime AA meetings. It was heartening to discover that she had been missed. In just the first few days, she was asked to lead meetings, asked to speak at a meeting, and asked to come over for a barbecue. She was reminded of the days of early sobriety, when she'd been able to attend one or two meetings a day and had felt a heady rush of joy to be, for the first time in a long, long while, fully cognizant again. Life was very rosy in her early days, and her newfound faith had been a source of deep comfort. Maybe, this summer, she could re-discover the joy.

Checking email midweek, she was pleased to receive an offer from the Glendale English Department for a second fall class. That gave her a full slate. Prayer answered! Quickly, she sent back her acceptance in a reply.

Soon it was Friday. Emily and Marianne had made plans to meet at the big speaker meeting. Emily decided to wear a black silk tee shirt with a long, brown and black patterned cotton skirt that had, thankfully, an elastic waist. She left early so she'd be able to find parking near the church where the meeting was held. Still, when she arrived, there was a large crowd gathered outside, smoking and sipping coffee and talking.

She spotted Marianne in conversation with a tall man with a jaunty goatee and went to join them.

"Emily, good, you made it. Do you know Ed?"

"Ed McGowan," he introduced himself, extending his hand. "Welcome to the meeting. You haven't been here before, have you? I'm sure I would have remembered."

Flattered, Emily explained that, during the summer, she usually went to daytime meetings.

"Ed's the Speaker Chair," Marianne clarified.

"That's a big job. How do you find people to come talk?"

"Well, Central Office provides a list. I use it if I want a circuit speaker. But I prefer to scout out local talent on my own. I get to lots of speaker meetings in the area, and if I like what someone has to say, I ask for his or her phone number. I also like to alternate man, woman."

"That's a good policy. Thanks for arranging for the evening's entertainment."

"You're most welcome. I enjoy the job. How about you? Do you speak yourself?"

"I do, on occasion. I'm actually speaking in Alhambra next week. A Baptist church near Alhambra and Main, Thursday night."

"I'd like to come hear you. I still have openings this summer. What time?"

"8:30."

"I'll be there, front row center. Now if you'll excuse me, I have to go make sure that tonight's speaker has everything she needs."

"Ed's a good guy," commented Marianne. "I think he likes you."

"Too early to tell. But he is cute. He isn't married?"

"Divorced, with a couple kids in college. I think they and his ex-wife live in Oregon now. So he's available."

"How long have you known him?"

"Oh, for years now. He and Alex used to hang out together, when Alex was still coming to meetings. They'd go to sporting events together. If he comes to hear you speak, make sure to pay attention to him."

"I'll make nice."

"I saved us a couple of seats. Shall we go claim them?"

"Sure."

They moved into the barn-like church hall, where folding chairs had been set up. Emily was glad to note that they had padded seats. Otherwise, it would be a long and uncomfortable hour and a half. While Marianne reclaimed her keys and held their place, Emily went to get herself a coffee and Marianne a refill. Cookies? Better not. They looked store bought, so why waste the calories.

The meeting got underway. Readings from the Big Book and then birthdays.

"They make a big deal out of birthdays here," Marianne whispered.

DENISE B.

Sure enough, everyone who was celebrating a sober anniversary came up to the podium and said a few words. "I'd like to thank God and all of you for my sobriety" was a common theme. After what must have been ten birthdays, the leader announced a break.

"Let's go outside and have a smoke," Marianne said, stretching. They headed back out to the courtyard, and Emily saw why the meeting was nicknamed the Meat Market. Crowds of young people were flirting and gesturing widely, showing off to each other and moving from group to group for maximum exposure. Emily chuckled to watch the show.

"Imagine getting sober that young. They have their whole lives ahead of them."

"They do, if they make it. And I hope they do."

Emily spotted Ed waving to them. She and Marianne strolled over to where he was standing next to a redhead almost as tall as he. She had her hair back in a French twist and was wearing a black linen dress and pearls. Very elegant, Emily thought, and was glad she'd taken care with her own appearance.

"I'd like you to meet our speaker for tonight, Molly B. She came out here from La Canada."

Emily and Marianne introduced themselves and shook hands.

"Thanks for making the drive, Molly. I look forward to hearing you tonight," Emily said.

"Oh well, it's not that far. Once I was asked to go out to Riverside. Now that was a long drive home. But we're supposed to 'go to any lengths,' right?"

"That's true."

They were joined by a man who looked very athletic. He was already tan for its being so early in the summer; his chest and arm muscles were clearly defined. He had a buzz cut and piercing blue eyes.

"Hi, I'm John," he introduced himself. "And you must be our speaker?"

"That I am. Pleased to meet you, John."

John looked like he approved. "Just tell the truth," he advised, "and go easy on the God angle."

Molly smiled. "Thanks for the tip."

As John moved away, Ed snorted. "There's an expert in every crowd. Don't let him intimidate you, Molly."

"Oh, I won't. I'll hold my own up there. Is it time to go back in?"

"Yep. Just about that time."

Everyone began to file back into the hall. Emily estimated that there must be about 300 people here tonight. Molly must be an experienced speaker.

Indeed, she proved to be. She told the story of being raised in San Marino to marry Mr. Right and how she followed that pattern by marrying a high-powered attorney. Feeling pressured to entertain, she lapsed into binge drinking and pill taking. After repeated cajolings and threats, her husband finally divorced her and got custody of their three children. Disgusted, her family shut her out.

After a life of wealth and privilege, she moved into a squat with other addicts and alcoholics. Penniless, she took to wearing a coat with deep inside pockets that she used to fill with stolen bottles of bourbon. She hit one market one too many times, and she was jailed for shoplifting. In jail, shaky and sick and weak, she went to a panel given by members of AA's Hospitals and Institutions Committee. There, she heard the message of sobriety from a woman who came from a similar background.

The woman gave her a copy of the Big Book, which she read with trembling hands. Inside the front cover was the woman's phone number. Once released, she called the number and to her amazement the woman came, picked her up, and took her to a meeting.

She didn't want to return to the squat. The woman set her up with a sleeping bag and let her sleep in a hammock in her backyard. Gradually, she felt ready to work and got a job as a checker at the same market she'd shoplifted from. That was ten years ago. Today, she was on good terms with her children and saw them often. She was a new grandmother and was trusted to babysit. She'd found love again and was happily re-married. Women frequently asked her to sponsor them, and she took them through the 12 steps as they had been taught to her.

DENISE B.

"Without sobriety, I have nothing. With it, I'm able to lead a happy, productive life. I'm Molly B, alcoholic. Thanks for listening."

Molly sat down to loud applause and the meeting was over.

Marianne and Emily got in line to thank the speaker. Emily's first sponsor had told her, "Always thank the speaker, no matter what you think of the job he did. That's a person who's just poured his heart out, so take the time to thank him."

"Want to hook up with some people and go out for coffee or dessert?" Marianne asked.

"No, not tonight. I've been getting up early lately. Must be a holdover from getting up to teach. I'm going to turn in."

"Okay. See you soon."

It had been a great Friday evening, Emily mused on the drive home. Funny to imagine how once, Friday evening would automatically mean all night at the bar, getting drunker and drunker and hoping for a handsome stranger to come along and offer her a fairy tale life. Well, tonight she'd met a handsome stranger in Ed. Wonder if that would go anywhere? Way to soon to tell.

The next morning, Emily once again awoke early and decided to start a good new summer habit of walking. She didn't aim to be as thin as Marianne, but she would like to get in better shape. She mapped out a route: up a long block to Garfield Park, through the park, across to Garfield, down to Oxley, and back home. That should be a decent workout, and she'd get to admire people's gardens along the way.

In the park, she veered off the pathway and into what she thought of as semi-wilderness, an overgrown area full of trees and bushes. Wilderness reminded her of James, the guy she still had a semi-crush on. Maybe someday he'd decide he wanted company when he camped.

On its side by one large bush was an almost empty bottle of bourbon.

"So. Someone made a night of it." As she bent down to pick up the bottle and put it in the trash, she saw a flash of white. Parting the bush, she leaned in to investigate. There, lying in a small clearing, was a naked woman, badly battered. Slowly, she gazed upward to the woman's face. It was Molly B.

Chapter Three

Reeling backward, Emily leaned into the bush to support herself. Years of reading mysteries had instilled in her the knowledge that she must not touch anything. She made her way to the nearest bench and sat down hard. Thank God she'd brought her purse with her. Now, was the cell phone charged? Yes. Trembling, she dialed 9-1-1.

South Pasadena was a small town, and she spotted police cars within minutes. She made her way to the curb to meet them and escort them to Molly's body. Once she'd shown them her gruesome discovery, an officer led her away.

"All right, miss. If you would sit down over there by the far picnic table. A detective will want to interview you."

Emily folded her arms on the table and lay her head down. She was chilled in the early morning cool. She was also profoundly shocked. Molly had been so vibrant just last night, so poised as she told her story of triumph. How had she ended up here? Had she never gone home? Had she been followed and abducted? Unbelievably, had she decided to get drunk and met up with a violent bum? Shuddering, she saw again the bruises that covered Molly's body. Someone had been ferociously, viciously angry. But who? And why? She huddled alone with her thoughts as she waited for what felt like a very long time. She was aware of a purposeful flurry of activity in the park's wilderness and supposed it would be the forensics people and the medical examiner.

She felt a gentle touch on her shoulder and looked up into the kind brown eyes of a female detective. Standing next to her was a sturdy man with a thick mustache.

"Ms. Davies? I'm Luz Gutierrez, and this is my partner Detective Hansen. We're from the Sheriff's Department. Do you feel up to answering some questions?"

"Yes. Whatever I can do."

"I understand that you recognized the victim. Did you know her well?"

Emily explained the situation. What she knew wasn't much. There had been, she estimated, 300 people who'd last seen Molly. Sometimes people went out after an AA meeting, and she did not know if that had been the case here.

The detectives, while kind to her, did not volunteer any information. She didn't really expect them to. After all, she was just the one who'd stumbled on the body. Luz Gutierrez gave her a card and asked her to call if anything else occurred to her. She hoped something would, but she doubted it. While she'd listened to Molly bare her soul, she'd only met her the one time.

"I'm free to go, then?"

"Yes. We may need to contact you again. You're understandably in shock right now. We can have an officer escort you home."

"It's just a block. I think I can make it."

"Nevertheless."

So Emily got a ride for the long block from the park to her cottage. It was a relief to see her own door and the wreath of dried flowers Marianne had given her as a housewarming gift. Marianne. She might be home, and she might be able to come over.

An hour later, the two friends were sitting at the table on Emily's back patio with steaming mugs of coffee. Gradually, the horror gave way to practical questions.

"How on earth will the police investigate? They'll never be able to track down everyone who was there last night. Even if they go to next Friday's meeting, the people attending change every week. Well, there are regulars, but you know what I mean."

"It is a daunting task, but they seemed very competent. Molly must have gone out with someone after the meeting, someone she trusted."

"You found that bottle first. Do you really think she went out after speaking and got drunk? It seems incredible."

"They'll do an autopsy and find out. It's possible, I suppose. If she was drunk, she wouldn't be able to fight back or just run away. Maybe someone forced her to drink it. Held her at knife point or something. Still, the question remains: why was it important to the killer that she be drunk?"

"Are the police going to let you know what they find out?"

"I doubt it. Why would they? It's not like I'm family or a close friend of Molly's. You know what gets to me the most is my own experience with violence. All those years of drinking, choosing violent men. When I first saw Molly lying there, before I realized who she was, I thought, 'This could so easily have happened to me.' I spent a lot of time in parks when I was homeless."

"Yes, that really brings it home."

Marianne insisted on staying the day. Working with what she found in Emily's fridge, she made them salads for lunch and then raided the shelves for ingredients for a tuna casserole for dinner. It was rich and creamy: comfort food.

"Thanks so much for coming over. I couldn't have done this day alone. Images of Molly would have haunted me the entire time."

"I was glad to do it, but I really have to get back to Alex now. Why don't you call your pastor and his wife? I know you're fond of them, and I'll bet they'd be willing to come over. I don't want you to be alone."

The Hendricks did indeed come. They listened to and prayed with Emily and invited her to come sleep over at their place.

"That way you won't have to be by yourself with nightmares," Jane urged. "And we have an extra bedroom no one's using."

"Do come," added the pastor. "Then we can go to church together in the morning."

"Oh thank you, but I'll be okay here. The shock is wearing off, and I don't think anyone is going to break in and nab me. It was wonderful of you to come."

Drained, Emily went to bed early. As she snuggled under the comforter, she thought of her long fascination with mysteries. The heroines always recovered quickly from finding dead bodies. Some, indeed, made a habit of it and were always stumbling across corpses. Then they jumped right in and solved the crime. She, in contrast, felt baffled and helpless. Who could have done it? What could she do to help?

That night she dreamed of Molly. She visited a room that housed victims of violence. Nicole Simpson was there, Molly was there, and every woman who'd been beaten to death. They rose up as one and, naming their attackers, begged for vengeance. They began to keen, an eerie sound that filled the room.

Emily awoke with a start. The keening was still echoing in her ears. She remembered no names, only the existence of the room, and it seemed so real. She realized that she'd had a visitation, and resolved that whatever she could do for justice, she would do.

At church that morning, Pastor Hendricks asked prayer for Molly and her family and friends and that the killer be apprehended. The praise band was back, and they'd chosen one of Emily's favorite choruses, "Nothing Is Impossible to Thee."

"Nothing, nothing absolutely nothing, nothing is impossible to Thee…" Emily felt her helplessness slip away, to be replaced with confidence.

Because she'd skipped a meeting the day before, after church Emily decided to make the short drive up to the War Memorial Building. She wouldn't stay for the main speaker, but she could visit with others and hear the readings and the ten-minute speaker.

At the meeting, she discovered that word of Molly's death had already spread. The commonplace comparison of rumor to a brush fire came to mind. The main story, as far as she could make out, seemed to be that Molly had gone to a liquor store, picked up a bottle and a stranger, gotten drunk, had a fight with him, and been killed by him.

She wanted to scream, "You know nothing about it!" She wanted to defend Molly, but she had no real facts to back up an assertion of innocence. Word that she had been the one to discover the body had not yet spread, so she was spared questions, for which she was grateful. She really did not want to repeat details.

As she was getting ready to leave at break, she saw Ed McGowan, Friday night's speaker chair, approach. She braced herself.

"Hi, Emily. Really sad day. I can't get my mind around it, you know? I can't imagine she'd drink, and I can't imagine she'd just stand still while someone beat her."

"No. The whole thing's incredible, really."

"I can't help but think, if only I'd insisted on picking her up at home, taking her to the meeting, and driving her back. I often do that, chauffeur the speakers. If I had, she'd still be alive."

"You can't blame yourself."

"No, but…hard not to. Listen, you mentioned that you were speaking this week. Was it Wednesday night?"

"Thursday. 8:30, at a Baptist Church on the corner of Main and Olive in Alhambra. Do you still want to come?"

"I really do. I'd love to hear you. Think of it as an audition."

Despite herself, Emily laughed. "All right. I hope I get the part."

Driving home, she felt lighter. He was only coming, of course, as part of an AA job. Still, it had felt good to bask in his attention. It had sure been a long time since she'd been involved with someone. Did she even remember how to go about it? Probably, she decided, she'd never learned in the first place.

For lunch she re-heated some tuna casserole and enjoyed it. Marianne had made a real cream sauce, instead of dumping in a can of mushroom soup. It was delicious. Then she decided to take care of a few loose ends.

WIDE OPEN

Dear Katharine,
    While I appreciate your thoughtfulness in bringing me the newspaper *Education Reporter*, I need you to stop giving me your copy. It's just too right wing for me. The June issue, which links a student's killing rampage with the fact that he studied with liberal English teachers, strikes me as really irresponsible.
    Thanks for all you do at church. You are indispensable. I'll see you next Sunday.
    Best,
    Emily

    There. That ought to buy her a little peace of mind. She had to admit that being so upset over the article had generated an article of her own. What to do with it? Why not send it in to the journal for community colleges? It had to do with students and teaching, after all. She'd do it.
    She spent the rest of the day with Elizabeth George, good company. In the evening, since she'd had a big lunch, she made a fruit salad and took it out to the patio. There! A hummingbird! Flash of color. She'd have to remember to tell Dad.
    Monday morning brought some early time with Irene, who asked prayer that her beautician's license be renewed. Living as she did out of town, she hadn't heard a thing about Molly's murder, which was refreshing. As the others arrived, though, Molly became the topic of discussion. Once again, it was assumed that Molly had gotten drunk and been killed by a drinking buddy.
    "After all, the homeless kill each other over a bottle of Ripple."
    "That must be it—a fatal slip."
    Emily bit her tongue. She was convinced of Molly's innocence but had no proof.

    Monday afternoon, Luz Gutierrez and Fred Hansen met with their lieutenant, James Roberts, at the Sheriff's Homicide Division in the City of Commerce. Roberts began.

"So let's review what we've got so far. Autopsy results are in. Relatives have been contacted. Initial interviews have been conducted. Let's start with the autopsy."

Fred consulted his notes. "No defensive wounds at all, indicating she was unconscious when the battery occurred. Slight bruising on the neck suggests she may have been gripped in a choke hold, cutting off circulation to the brain."

"Would that really have knocked her out long enough for the battery to take place?" asked Luz skeptically.

"Long enough to get started. It was actually the battery that killed her."

"Likely weapon?"

"Something consistent with a baseball bat."

"Stomach contents?"

"Partially digested lemon pie. And the lab work showed almost a quart of bourbon."

"Okay, the bourbon would certainly have made her unconscious. And the pie?"

"Witnesses confirm she did go out with a party of four to Conrad's Restaurant after speaking at the meeting. She never made it back to her car; it was impounded from the restaurant's parking lot Saturday after being there all night. Meeting ended at 9:30 Friday night. She left the restaurant around 10:30. Estimated time of death, 10:30 to midnight."

Luz took over. "We've spoken with the group who went to Conrad's. Apparently they go every Friday night for dessert or a late meal. They always invite the speaker. They say she was the first to leave, which their waitress confirms."

"And you took care of the family?" asked Roberts.

"Two families. She was divorced and remarried. The ex is an attorney, lives in Arcadia. Was out with a client, who confirms. He was almost as broken up as the current spouse. Apparently they'd mended their fences. They had three kids, youngest twenty, attends UCLA. The two oldest married, one with a baby. Both were home that night."

"And the current husband?"

"One Jason Brannigan. Real estate agent. Had already placed a call to report her missing and had himself called the local hospitals. Took it hard. Spent Friday night home alone; never went along when she went out to meetings. Says she kept that part of her life separate."

"Anything to suggest he followed her? Was jealous or suspicious of her AA life?"

"Of course it's possible. You want us to follow up on that? Re-interview him?"

"Him and anyone who might have a take on their marriage."

"Okay. So what we've got: vic goes to meeting, speaks, is a big hit. Drives herself to Conrad's. Stays roughly 45 minutes. Leaves alone and never makes it to her car."

Ed took over. "So the perp must have followed her from the meeting. Transported her to the park. Looks like the attack took place in the park itself."

"And the people who live overlooking the park?"

"Initial canvas: none of the neighbors heard or saw a thing."

"Too bad. One more thing."

"What's that?"

"Let's find that baseball bat."

Monday evening, Emily decided to go to Monday Night Mumblers. It was another meeting she could never get to when she was working. She arrived early, and there as always was Zack, who'd been taking care of set-up for as long as she'd known him.

"Welcome back! You must be off for the summer."

"That I am. It's good to be back."

"Horrible thing with Molly B. I understand you found her."

So, the word was out. She didn't even bother to wonder how. Sensing her discomfort, Zack did not probe, for which she was grateful.

"I was probably one of the last ones to see her alive, or so the police think. They interviewed me yesterday. Our usual group went out to Conrad's, where we take the speaker."

"How did she seem then?"

DENISE B.

"Upbeat. She could tell everyone had enjoyed her talk. She was full of stories about her new grandchild, how much it meant to be trusted with him. Showed us pictures. And now she's gone. Just like that. I really hope they catch whoever killed her. She was a fine lady."

"That she was."

There were about forty people at Mumblers that night. The format of the meeting was that people could write anonymous questions and put them in a basket. The leader then read the questions out loud, and anyone from the floor could answer. Emily usually found it entertaining, as there were a variety of answers.

That night, after the typical questions about how to find a sponsor and how, exactly, to find a Higher Power when one did not believe, came this one: "How do you make amends?"

The first hand to shoot up belonged to John W. Emily recognized him at once as the muscled man with the buzz cut who'd come up to meet Molly B. Friday night.

"I know about amends. I used to get drunk every weekend, come home, and beat up my wife. A couple times, I put her in the hospital. When I got sober, I wrote her a long letter of apology and begged forgiveness."

Emily bridled. Her hand shot up too. After a few more responses, the leader called on her.

"I've been a victim of domestic violence. And I would like an amends made to me. But I would not like the perpetrator to just apologize and beg my forgiveness. I would like him to say, 'I was totally wrong and you never deserved it. You never did one thing to deserve it. I'll stay out of your life, and I'll hope and pray that you heal.'"

She knew her answer came very close to cross-talk, directly responding to someone else's comment. Cross-talk was discouraged. But she didn't care. John, she noticed, sent her a dirty look. Well, good. He'd gotten the message.

There was no break at Mumblers, so after the first 45 minutes Emily slipped outside to join the other smokers.

"Guess you really told John off," grinned a young woman whose name, Emily thought, was Cathy.

"Well, I couldn't stand the image his answer conjured up. Begging forgiveness indeed. I was in one brief, bad marriage where the guy used to beat me up, actually throwing me against walls. After his violent fits he'd always get super remorseful and even go down on his knees, crying, asking me to forgive him. It made me really, really angry."

"I'd like to see the guy who'd try and hit me," Cathy boasted. "I'd give as good as I got. Then when he fell asleep I'd bash him with a frying pan. That's what my mother used to do. She was one peppery lady."

Emily laughed. "Well, I hope you never have to use that particular skill. But it's good to know that you're prepared."

Back inside, Emily was in time to hear one of her favorite answers. The question had been, "How do you take a moral inventory?" Zack loved to respond to that one: "I took the inside of a matchbook cover and wrote, 'I was a liar, a cheat, and a thief.' My sponsor said, 'Great. Now your inventory's done. Let's move on.'"

Back home, she wondered if she'd dream about the Victims' Room again. How she wanted to help them. How she wanted justice for them. She sent a special prayer for the detectives working the case. How she wanted them to triumph.

She had Luz Gutierrez's card, but she could hardly call to tell her about a dream. Anyway, although the dream women had named their killers, she could not remember any names. No, all she remembered was their dreadful keening.

Well, she hadn't checked her email yet. There were no new messages, but she couldn't postpone telling her mother about Molly's murder.

"Hi there, Mom. Don't panic, but I found a dead body Saturday morning. It turned out to be a woman in AA whom I'd just heard speak the night before. I didn't know her, but I really liked her from what she revealed in her talk. Anyway, there are a couple of good detectives on the case. I hope that, like in our favorite mysteries, they quickly solve it. I figure the killer has got to be either someone from her home life or someone from the meeting. Don't know why, except the 'random stranger' idea seems so unlikely.

DENISE B.

"Hope you and Nick are enjoying Santa Barbara. Do let me know when the sun comes out. I'd enjoy getting out of town for a few days now that I'm off work. Talk with you soon. Love, Emily."

There, message sent. It would be interesting to hear her mother's response. She was usually very level-headed.

Emily got ready for bed and crawled in, propping herself up on pillows so she could read a few more chapters of George's book. It was often re-read, so she knew of course who the killer was, and this time through she looked carefully for any clues George might have strewn.

As she turned out the light, she remembered to thank God for another sober day and to review the day, briefly, just for things done right and wrong. Right: well, she'd gotten to two meetings. And she'd been given a chance to articulate her views on violent men. Wrong: in doing so, she'd been guilty of specific cross-talk and had definitely alienated John. Did she owe an amends? It had felt so good to give her own point of view! Still, maybe she did. She'd sleep on it.

Chapter Four

Tuesday morning, after coffee and prayers, the phone rang. Emily had to hustle into the cottage from the patio to pick up before it went to the answering machine.

"Hello?"

"Hi, hon, it's Mom. Did I wake you?"

"Oh no, I was up. Good morning. You got my email, I take it."

"I sure did, and I want to hear all about this body you discovered. The sun has emerged up here. Why don't you drive up and stay a few days?"

Emily thought. She could just manage it.

"I have to be back by Thursday night, but it sounds possible."

"If you leave this morning, you'll have the rest of the day, all Wednesday, and still have plenty of time to get back in time for your appointment."

"Sounds doable."

"Great. The guest room is all ready for you. Nick would love to see you too. So later today?"

"Yep. I'll leave in about an hour."

"See you soon, then."

Rejoicing that she now had the freedom to take a short trip whenever she wanted, Emily quickly ate, showered, and dressed. The sun was out, so denim shorts and her red tee. Packing was easy: bathing suit, her light green pants and top to wear in case they went out to dinner, underthings, toiletries. Was she forgetting anything? Ah, mail.

DENISE B.

She walked back out through the patio to knock on her landlady's back door. Jean, who suffered with arthritis, was usually up earlier than she. Sure enough, Jean opened the door.

"Ah, Emily. Good morning. I was just making another pot of tea. Care to join me?"

"I'd love to another time. I've just decided to make an impromptu trip up to Santa Barbara and wondered if you'd be willing to pick up my mail so it doesn't clog the box."

"Oh, of course. You've done it for me countless times. Don't worry about a thing, and do have a good time."

There. No pets to board, no timers to activate: she was ready to go. Wait! She'd forgotten a book for the beach. The George mystery was long, and she'd only gotten about a third of the way through. That would be perfect.

Emily headed west through town to catch the freeway. This was a familiar route; she'd taken it every morning spring semester to get to work. Today she drove with a light heart; the trip was purely for fun.

As she made her way to the 101 North, she reflected on her parents. They'd divorced when she was in college, telling her that they'd stayed together so that she'd have a stable home life growing up. While the news had been startling at the time, she'd soon learned that her father's late nights at the office were really a series of romances, and that her mother had wearied of his roving eye.

Now he was happily ensconced in a retirement community in San Francisco, single, able to flirt with whomever he chose for as long as he chose. And her mom, who'd wasted no time in finding another husband, had now been with Nick for...what was it? She did a mental calculation. Must be going on 37 years now.

Nick was a widower who had attended Mom's church, and she'd asked him to go to the symphony with her, claiming to have an "extra ticket." In turn, he'd asked her to dinner. After a brief courtship they'd married. Those early years of marriage had been rough as her mom discovered that Nick was an alcoholic. But he'd responded to her ultimatum, get help or I leave you, by joining AA. And by the time Emily accepted that she needed help with drinking, he'd been able to act as her guide.

It took an hour and a half to make the drive this morning. She'd missed commuter traffic, which was headed in the other direction. She took the first Santa Barbara exit, Cabrillo, and exulted at the view of the ocean it provided. Blue and sparkly. The street curved around the beaches and then uphill to the bluffs. Emily turned on Cliff Drive and was able to park right in front of their home.

She noticed baby tomatoes growing out front. Those would be delicious. As she walked up the pathway, her mother opened the door.

"Welcome! You made good time."

At 86, Ruth Paulson could have passed for a woman in her sixties. Golf and water aerobics kept her in excellent shape. Her white hair, excellently cut and shaped, contrasted nicely with a light tan.

Emily hugged her mother.

"Yes, I missed the traffic. So, here I am. Ready to be pumped about the body."

Ruth laughed. "No, I just couldn't resist your email. I've never met anyone who discovered a body before. Read about it plenty, but never in real life. But come in, say hi to Nick."

Nick, born in England, still kept a trace of an accent. With silver hair and mustache, a cane he loved to twirl, and a six-four frame, he was an imposing figure. Emily kissed him on the cheek.

"What are you listening to these days, Nick?" His macular degeneration necessitated books on tape, a Godsend since he'd been an avid reader all his life.

"*War and Peace*. Never did get around to it before. It's as good as its reputation. We've been listening to it together. I figure it will last all summer."

"Are you keeping the characters straight?"

"At first those names gave me some trouble, but now the characters are drawn and it's fairly easy to recognize who's who. How was the drive up?"

"Easy. I always look forward to that first glimpse of the ocean."

"We thought we'd head out to the beach after lunch, if you'd like. Not sure how long you can stay."

"This trip is a short one. Thought I'd head back tomorrow night after dinner."

"Yes, you're speaking, Ruth said. I'd like to hear you. Maybe next trip you can stay longer and we can arrange to have you speak at one of the meetings here."

"Sounds good. I always give you a plug, you know, as the one who introduced me to AA and prayed for me to get here."

"Sure, I'll take credit for that."

"Emily, if you'd go pick a few tomatoes, I'll get lunch ready. I thought we'd have salade Nicoise on the patio," Ruth said.

"Sounds marvelous."

After savoring lunch, with its chunks of tuna, tomato, olives, capers, and hard-boiled eggs (which Emily pushed to the side of the plate), they headed for Arroyo Burro beach, a short drive away. It was a small family-oriented beach, quite different from the bigger tourist beaches farther south. They set up a large umbrella and chairs up against the rocks with a good view of the ocean. Emily gazed out at the sun sparkling on the water, always a magical sight. The breakers, with their white froth, lulled her into a sense of peace and contentment.

"So. I've been very patient. Now tell all. Where was the body, who was it, and who do you think did it?"

Laughing at her mother's avid curiosity, Emily described the scene. In this setting, with sun and water and loved ones, the discovery lost its horror. Sadness remained, but with it came a sense of detachment.

"So you knew not to touch the bottle of bourbon."

"Right. But I don't know if the cops were able to lift any prints."

"Should be a good surface, if there were any. I suppose the big question is, did she drink again and thereby indirectly cause her own death."

"Blame the victim, you mean? Yeah, there's a lot of that going around at meetings. That she gave in to an overwhelming urge and then was killed by a drinking partner. Somehow I doubt it, though. Having heard her, it seemed to me that her sobriety was solid."

"Drunk or sober," intoned Nick, who had appeared to be dozing, "no one deserves to die like that." Tacitly, Ruth and Emily agreed to let him have the last word.

After a few hours of beach, they headed home to rinse off the sand and get ready for dinner. They'd decided to go out to Enterprise Fish Company, a favorite. Emily drove them down State, parked by the train station, and they made their way into the restaurant. They were pleased to get a table on the raised dais by the aquarium, where the din of silverware and raised voices was lessened. Emily chose swordfish with rice pilaf, Ruth the crab cakes, and Nick the sea bass.

"If you want to fit in a meeting while you're here," said Nick, "there's a good small discussion meeting tonight near the Mission. That is, if you don't mind driving. I'd love to show you off."

"As your prize student? Sure, that would be fun. Let's go."

So it was that after dinner and dropping Ruth off, she and Nick made their way to the meeting.

"Nick, you old dog. Did you ditch Ruth for a new trophy wife?" called out a portly man with pipe in hand.

"Rinse out your dirty mouth, Stan," said Nick, standing erect. "This is my daughter Emily." It warmed her heart to be identified as his daughter.

"My mistake. Sorry, Emily. Go on inside for coffee and cookies. We're just about ready to start."

The topic for discussion was finding God's will.

"For me," began Nick, "God's will came through my wife. We were newlyweds, and I'd never loved anyone so much. When she told me I had to choose between her and alcohol, that it was my life to ruin if I liked but she wasn't going to stick around to watch, I knew what I had to do."

"A good Alanon," murmured someone.

"I have a lot of trouble with this concept," admitted a woman who looked to be in her twenties. "The first time I set foot in a church was when I started coming to meetings. And the very word 'God' repulsed me at first. I was always taught to make my own way in the world. All I can say is, I guess it's God's will for me to stay sober. Beyond that, I have no clue."

Emily raised her hand and was called on. "I'd ended up a homeless drunk at the end, right here in Santa Barbara, where the missions are good. Panhandling was pretty good too. I'd lost all contact with my family. I didn't know that my mother used to wake up in the middle of the night, fearing I was lying in a ditch, wounded or dead. I didn't know that Nick was praying for me every night to get sober. But in spite of me, those prayers worked. One day, I just decided to go home and get help.

"Since then, I've discovered that when I'm following God's will, everything goes smoothly. When things get sticky and rough, it means I'm trying to do it on my own."

The meeting was only an hour. As things were breaking up, Nick motioned to a woman with huge blue-rimmed glasses and a matching blue sundress.

"Phoebe, this is my daughter Emily. She'll be coming up here a lot over the summer. Any chance of getting her to speak at the Sunday meeting?"

"Hi, Emily. Sounds like you have a good story. Let me give you my card. I arrange for speakers Sunday, and I'd love to hear you when you're in town. Just give me a few weeks notice."

"I'm sure we can work something out, Phoebe. I'll give you a call."

When they returned to the house, Ruth was getting ready for bed and Emily too was tired. The guest room had its own bath, so there was no waiting, and she was soon asleep.

The next morning, over a breakfast of freshly squeezed orange juice, coffee, and croissants, Ruth began to plan the day.

"You're the guest, so what would you like to do? There's more beach, shopping, the Mission, the Bird Refuge…"

"More beach. Then tonight I'd like to take you both to dinner at the Montecito Inn. If we take two cars, I can head home from there."

"Sounds like a good plan. I'll make us a reservation."

Once again, they headed for the beach, which was nearly empty this morning. After setting up umbrella and chairs to hold a spot, they decided to take a walk along the damp sand near the water's edge. One direction was for dogs off the leash; the other required leashes.

"Let's go to the right. I don't want to be sprayed by an exuberant animal just out of the surf," declared Ruth. So they ambled along, admiring driftwood, shells, and a wonderful cave.

"That would make a good hideout for a hermit," Emily speculated.

"I'm sure it's been used that way."

"And for courting couples," Nick suggested.

By the time they'd again reached the umbrella, the sun was quite hot, and Emily decided to take a swim. It was cold at first, as she plunged in, and then warmed to body temperature. Invigorated, she used the crawl, getting far enough out to avoid the dogs. She rested, floating on her back, feeling buoyant and free, and then rode a wave back in, landing where the toddlers were splashing and playing.

When she returned, Ruth was deep into a cooking mystery by Joanne Fluke, and Nick was on the lookout, he said, for women in bikinis. Apparently his bad eyesight did not prevent him from enjoying female pulchritude.

Emily read more of the George novel, then picked up chili dogs for their lunch from the stand by the beach. She made sure to add lots of napkins, as it was a goopy meal.

Sated, they agreed to head back for afternoon naps before tea. Napping was a luxury Emily could not afford when she was teaching, so she happily lay her head on the lavender-scented pillow, waking in a couple of hours to find Ruth in the kitchen preparing the tea.

"It's a custom, of course, that Nick brought from England. In the early days of our marriage it was strange to me, but now I look forward to it. If you'll take the tray out to the patio, I'll bring this plate of macaroons."

The patio was surrounded by a colorful garden which Emily praised.

"Couldn't do it without our gardener. He comes every Monday and gets things into shape."

"He does a great job. So obviously you've adjusted well to the move to Santa Barbara."

"Best thing we've ever done. I missed my Pasadena friends at first, but we're close enough for them to come visit. And I found a new bridge group right away, lovely bunch of ladies. The golf course offers a nine-hole time slot for seniors, so I've made friends there. And Nick has made friends at meetings."

"You make retirement sound like a dream come true."

"You'll enjoy it too, when the time comes. How about your fall teaching schedule? Is that all set?"

"Oh, yes. I just got an email from Glendale offering me another course, so that brings the total up to five classes for fall. That's perfect. But I'm in no rush to get back."

"I'll bet murder was not in your summer plans."

"Heavens, no. That was an all-time shocker. The day I found her, I was a basket case. Then I began dreaming about it. Now, I'm just rooting for the detectives."

"So you think they're good?"

"They were wonderful with me. I'm sure they'll figure it out."

"They'll need all the skill they've got, what with a suspect base of 300 alcoholics to weed through. They can hardly hold them all in one room while they conduct interviews."

"No. I'm not sure how they'll handle that aspect of it. I'm guessing they'll be looking into her private life too."

"Naturally."

As evening closed in, they drove separately into Montecito to the inn which featured a cutout of Charlie Chaplin, a famous guest. Emily was grateful for the valet parking, since there was nothing on the street. There was no wait for a table; theirs was right by a window with a view to the street. Once inside, she and Nick both ordered the filet mignon while Ruth chose the duck.

"No one minds if I have a glass of wine?" Ruth asked, sure of the answer.

"Go right ahead, dear. Emily and I like to see a person who's able to enjoy a good drink."

When her wine arrived, Ruth proposed a toast. "Here's to crime solving!"

"To crime solving," echoed Emily and Nick, clinking their water glasses.

The service was excellent, and they were soon enjoying their meal. Nick beamed. "Here we are in elegant surroundings. Thank you for the treat. This is certainly a far cry from your homeless days."

"Indeed. Much preferable to a meal out of a Dumpster."

"Do you ever see your old homeless friends when you come here for a visit?" asked Ruth.

"No, they wouldn't be hanging out in your area. If I wanted to find them, I'd have to hit the liquor stores on lower State, the Fig Tree, and the parks. But I can't say as I want to see them again. I think it would be too sad. Also, truth be told, I'd be afraid to get lured back in to drinking with them."

"A clean break is best," Nick agreed.

After the meal, they made their goodbyes. Emily retrieved her car and began the trek south, again missing all traffic although she drove more slowly at night. By ten, she was back at the cottage. It had been a good getaway.

Chapter Five

By Thursday morning, Emily felt completely in the rhythm of summer vacation. Her leisure time was a pleasure. Santa Barbara had been fun, and she'd go again. Back home, the morning fog had completely cleared, and the day was sunny and warm.

Once again, she decided on a morning walk. Today, she would avoid the park and head south. She took Monterey all the way to Garfield, down to Oak, then back to Oxley and up to her cottage. Oak was her favorite street. Lined with the trees that were a landmark in South Pasadena, the street contained graceful homes and lovely gardens. She was grateful to those homeowners who took such care with their front yards as to give pleasure to passersby. The only hazards were the places in the sidewalk where big old tree roots had buckled the concrete.

Time to collect the mail. After thanking her landlady, she leafed through the collection. Ads, ads, ads…letter from EDD. Yes! She'd been approved for unemployment benefits. She'd get $405 a week: no fortune, but it would certainly help this summer.

Tonight, she'd speak at the meeting in Alhambra. She prayed that she'd have fun with it and say what people needed to hear and what she needed to say. She was a little nervous but remembered that she'd told her story many times and that indeed, once she got started, it would tell itself. That's the way it always worked; it must be the Spirit moving within.

WIDE OPEN

She wondered if Ed would really show. Was Marianne right about his being interested in her? Or was he just naturally friendly? To play it safe, she'd take extra care in dressing. She chose a pale yellow jersey dress that complemented her hair and eyes. A long azure beaded necklace and white sandals would complete the outfit.

She hoped she'd be able to keep herself awake. She usually was in bed by 9:00, and the meeting went from 8:30-10:00. She'd better take a nap after lunch. Lunch, she remembered, was Eddie Park today. She thought of that luncheon meeting as her home group, as it was the first place she'd admitted she was an alcoholic. Coming as it did in the middle of the day, she could never go when she was teaching, but now she was free.

Arriving early to help with set-up, she found Al making the coffee and iced tea. He was slightly deaf, so she had to make sure to greet him face to face. He was delighted to see her and directed her to the French bread he'd brought, which needed to be sliced and buttered.

After that chore, she put out the books and leaflets, amused to note that one was "to Teenagers." Most of the people at this meeting were retired seniors. There were precious few young people. Still, the unlikely had happened before.

Soon Zack arrived. "Glad to see I got here in time to miss all the work," he said with a smile. She and Al had already put up the tables and chairs.

"You do enough at Mumblers. How's it going today?"

"Fine if you don't want the details."

It was early yet, so Emily took a cup of iced tea out to the far corner of the porch, where the cigarette smoke would not drift into the room and bother people. She had to be super careful not to offend others with secondhand smoke. It was a far cry from the early days of AA, when ashtrays would be set out one or two per row of chairs and the air was soon thick with smoke.

From her position, she could watch everyone arrive down the long driveway, through the park, and into the meeting. She waved, acting as greeter. She was pleased to see Allison, a fireplug of a woman with bleached blonde hair who had worked for years as society editor for the *Times*. She knew all the watering holes in Los Angeles and loved to tell bar stories.

"Well, hello there, Emily," she said, her face lighting up with genuine pleasure. "It's been too long. How lovely to see you back with us. You're standing by yourself out here like a pariah."

"Trying not to offend anyone by smoking."

"I'd join you if I could, but my doctor told me in no uncertain terms that it was quit or use an oxygen tank, and I don't want to lug one of those things around."

"Certainly not. How have you been?"

"Fine, fine, except that it's getting to be time to put my dog down. We've been together for many years, and I'll miss her dearly. Still, she's old and tired and her body has just stopped working."

"I'm sorry, Allison. I know that will be hard."

"Well, yes. But the death of a pet pales beside the death of a fellow alcoholic. I was so shocked to hear about Molly B. I used to write about her way back when in the society pages. She came from a very prominent San Marino family, always involved in balls and charity fundraisers. I know they'll be taking it hard. They were so happy to welcome her back into the fold when she turned her life around."

"Oh yes, it was a terrible waste of a life."

"It's hard too to imagine that we might be harboring a killer in our midst. Because I don't believe the husband did it. He always struck me as ineffectual."

Emily laughed. "Well, that's one way to get off the hook."

"Mealtime!" yelled Al from inside the room.

"Let's go in—I'm starving."

Lunch was lasagna and salad with ice cream for dessert. The speaker had just celebrated 30 years sober and said how important it was for her to recall the days of her drinking. "I never want to forget the misery. Life is so good today, but if I forget, it's all over."

After the meeting she slept for an hour and awoke refreshed. The rest of the day passed quickly, and soon it was time to go. As she headed down Fremont into Alhambra, she remembered the last time she'd gone to the Baptist Church. There had been a shortage of college courses for her one semester, and she'd gotten hired by an outfit that tutored high school students in how to take the College Entrance Exam. What a nightmare that job had been! Pressure from parents who wanted their children to excel. Students who wanted to ace the exam without putting forth much effort. Pressure from her boss to keep the class lively and to produce results. She'd been so grateful when her colleges were once again able to offer her enough classes so that she could quit tutoring.

There must be a lot going on at the church tonight, she mused, as she pulled into the lot and saw all the cars. Fortunately, she spotted a place at the end and took it. After asking directions of a mother who held a small infant, she located the room.

She was early; the coffee maker was still setting up. Norton, who'd asked her to come speak, was already there and thanked her for coming. He was wearing his t-shirt with a design of praying hands and also sported a large metal cross. Now there was a guy who was not shy about his faith.

The coffee maker introduced herself. She was a stocky woman with an olive complexion and a mop of wild curly black hair. She was dressed in nurse's scrubs.

"Hi, I'm Sandy. Just got off a twelve-hour shift, so excuse my appearance. These days, I go in early. I tell them, I can't work late no more. I gotta be outta there by 6:00 to make my meetings."

"That shows real dedication."

"Yeah, about all I do these days is work and AA. I got almost two years, and I got a lotta commitments. I do coffee here, and I'm secretary at a Saturday meeting."

"Sounds like you've really jumped in with both feet."

"Yeah, that's what my sponsor says."

At that point, Emily looked up to see that Ed had arrived. He ambled over to greet her. She noticed once again how tall he was—about Nick's height. Tonight he was dressed casually in a Hawaiian shirt and jeans over his taut form.

"Had no trouble finding the place. Are you ready to take the podium?"

DENISE B.

"Sure, I'll be ready. Thanks for coming."

"Wouldn't miss it. Like I told you, I get to lots of speaker meetings so I can get names and numbers for Friday night. I'm really looking forward to hearing you. I'll sit right here up front. Can I get you anything? Coffee or water?"

"Thanks. I'll take a cup of decaf with creamer."

He busied himself behind the counter and returned with a cup for each of them.

"Here you go. When you get up there, just signal if you need another drink. Sometimes speakers get parched halfway through. I'll sneak up and bring you some water."

"Thanks. I'll let you know. Looking at the people coming in tonight, I notice a big gap. There seem to be quite a few oldtimers and then a big crowd of newcomers on court cards. I hope I can keep everybody's interest."

Ed scanned the church hall.

"You're right. You've got the old and the new here. Quite a challenge. But I'm sure you're up to it."

Norton, acting secretary, got the meeting started. Emily let the preliminaries wash over her as she readied herself for her talk.

"And now, coming from South Pasadena is our speaker tonight, Emily D."

She walked up to the podium and, ignoring the big microphone, stood in front of it. Years of high school drama plus years of teaching had taught her to project. Also, she liked to move around as she spoke. She plunged in.

"I believe that I was born an alcoholic. When I was a child, I used to play with dolls. I'd have the boy dolls sit in one room reading *Playboy* magazine. Then one of the girl dolls would say, 'Let's go to the bar!' All the girl dolls would pile in their car and head off to the bar. I'd move their little arms up and down as they drank.

"One day my mother came in and asked me what the dolls were doing. I told her they were at a bar. She was shocked. 'Emmy, no! Ladies don't go to bars by themselves!' I decided then and there that when I grew up, ladies *would* go to bars by themselves. And indeed, I was to do a lot of bar drinking.

"My actual drinking did not start until high school, when we'd ask Pasadena City College students to buy us beer for parties. My drinking then had two main effects: I'd either get very depressed and isolate, or I'd get very promiscuous and hop into bed with whomever asked me. The promiscuity made me feel very bad about myself, but the next weekend I'd repeat it. So a vicious cycle was begun.

"I continued to drink steadily all through college and grad school, but in those days I'd limit it to weekends. I'd study hard during the week and then drink to oblivion on the weekends. I did very well in school, but once I got out I was floundering. I knew how to impress teachers, but I was totally unprepared for real life.

"I worked a series of jobs, each less demanding than the previous one, each time getting fired for my drinking. Finally, I ended up in Sausalito and was taking in typing jobs. I could barely pay the rent. Each night, I'd know I had to have at least a dollar for that first draft beer at the local bar. After that, I could hustle drinks all night and bring someone home with me. One night, as I scanned the bar, I realized that I could not remember whom I'd already slept with.

"My landlord got fed up, and one day I came home to an eviction notice on the door. I knew then that I was on a real downhill slide. Indeed I was. I became a homeless alcoholic, and I was to remain one for the next ten years. I slept in abandoned cars, I panhandled for a bottle, I learned how to Dumpster dive.

"There were certain rules for panhandling. It was forbidden to usurp someone else's corner. Very territorial. It was okay to gather in a group in front of the supermarket and spread out into the parking lot, asking for spare change. That way, fairly quickly, we'd pool our earnings and have enough for a bottle. We'd scurry around to the back of the market and pass the bottle. We knew we had to keep a certain level of alcohol in our system in order to just maintain. I remember once being in the circle and standing next to a man who was shaky and sick. The others knew he'd let his alcohol level drop too low. 'Keep it down, brother!' they cried out. 'Keep it down!'

"I also discovered Dumpster diving. I'd find large Dumpsters near the fancier houseboats, because they had the best stuff. I'd climb the outside ridges to the top and then lower myself in. I'd gather whatever looked good—leftover pizza, pasta, salad ends—and then sink to the bottom where the bottles were. Most of the bottles still had a little left in them, what we called a 'spider.' I'd pour all the leftover wine into one bottle and all the hard liquor into another, chug it all down, and get the jump on the day.

"There was a lot of violence in the homeless crowd. The drunker we got, the louder we got and the more tempers would flare. One day I saw a man staggering down the street. He'd gotten hit with an empty wine bottle and had a large gash in his forehead, with blood streaming down his face.

"'Oh man,' I said. 'You'd better get to the hospital.'

"'No way,' he said. 'I've got to get to the liquor store.'

"I was unprepared for the violence. I'd been raised in a middle-class home where we were polite with one another. Now I was getting hit. I learned to run fast, to duck, and to fight myself. One fight I was winning, because my opponent was drunker than I was. I had him pinned to the ground and declared myself the winner. Then he, fighting dirty, lifted up his head and bit my ear, removing a chunk.

"There was also a lot of jail, especially when I migrated from Sausalito to Santa Barbara. Santa Barbara is a tourist town, and they like to keep it pretty and clean. No dirty homeless bums cluttering up the streets. So we'd get picked up all the time for drunk in public, illegal camping, and the like.

"It was in jail that I first ran into AA. A couple of ladies would come every week to the women's side and hold a meeting. It absolutely baffled me that they would voluntarily come to jail when they didn't have to be there. What I did pick up there was the Serenity Prayer: 'God, grant me the serenity to accept the things I cannot change, the courage to change the things I can, and the wisdom to know the difference.' Once I got out, I'd say that prayer over a bottle. I figured one thing I could not change was being an alcoholic, so I'd best accept it.

"What happened for me was a miracle. I'd migrated back up to San Francisco and was living in Golden Gate Park with a group. One night we got into a fight over whose turn it was to push the shopping cart, and I ended up getting hit. The next morning I had a huge black eye.

"My cohorts were dismayed. They knew that my SSI check would be coming in soon, and they needed to stay on my good side, because it was my habit to cash the check, hit the liquor store, and host a big party for a few days.

"'Em,' they said. 'Why don't you just take it easy today? You don't have to do any work. We'll take care of everything. You just pull your bedroll over by that tree and relax.'

"So I did. And when I came to, I had changed. I looked at the prone forms of my companions and I thought, 'What am I doing here? There's nothing holding me here. I think I'll walk away.' I did. As I walked, I felt a strong presence surrounding me. I asked, 'What is this?' I got the answer, 'This is prayer. There are a lot of people praying for you.' I decided not to question it. If this was my chance, I would take it.

"I found a shelter that night, and the next morning cashed the check. Instead of heading back to the park for a party, I went to the Greyhound bus station and got a ticket for Los Angeles.

"From there, I made it to my mother and stepfather's home, where I asked for help. They were delighted to see me. Through the years, my mother would wake up in the middle of the night, sure that I had been attacked and was dying and calling out to her. She was very happy to see me safe. It turned out that my stepfather was a member of AA, and he began taking me to meetings, one or two a day. He said he'd never been to so many meetings.

"I just let AA become my life in those days. I had no other life, after all. At one women's meeting, I asked a woman to be my sponsor. What I liked about her was that she laughed a lot and was comfortable with saying 'God.' She took me gradually through the steps, for which I am very grateful. On one's own, they are daunting. With help, they become doable and life-changing.

"After awhile, I realized I had to become self-supporting. At the time, I was working a volunteer job. My boss asked, 'Aren't you trained to be a teacher?' Yes, I was. He told me that his wife worked for the Community College District. He would ask her for an application, and she would walk it through the system.

"I got the application and began to fill it out. To my horror, one question was, 'Have you ever been arrested?' I figured that I had been jailed over a hundred times. I checked 'Yes' and wrote, 'See attached.' On a separate page, I wrote, 'I went through a rough battle with alcoholism and was often jailed for being drunk in public. I have now been sober for three years and have made a new life for myself. I hope this sordid episode will not prejudice you from hiring me.'

"It worked. I got the job. And I've been working as a college English teacher ever since. I love the work, and one of the best things about it is getting summers off. When I'm working, I'm only able to get to two or three meetings a week. By the end of the semester, I notice I'm pretty high strung and frazzled. Now summer is here, I can get back into the swing of meetings, and for that I'm grateful.

"Thank you for being here tonight, and thank you for listening."

As Emily sat down, Ed leaned over and kissed her on the cheek. "That was marvelous," he whispered. He waited while others came up to thank her.

"I'd really like you to come speak for me some Friday night. I've got July booked, but what about August?"

"I can do that."

"Great. Let me get your number."

He then insisted on walking her to her car. As they said good night, he kissed her on the lips, just the lightest, most gentle touch. "See you tomorrow night?"

"Yes. I'll be there."

On the drive home, she replayed the kiss in her mind. It had been so light, she almost could have imagined it. When she arrived home, she saw she had a message. It was Marianne.

"Hey there. Remembered you were speaking tonight. I know you'll do great. Are we on for this Saturday? It's my turn to pick the place and I thought maybe that pizza place on Lake. And how about tomorrow night? Are you up for the big meeting, or would it be too traumatic. Let me know."

There was a second message from her father. "Got your letter. Thanks a lot. I'm glad you're off for the summer. Would love to have you come up for a visit. I'm free any time. Call and we can set something up. Love you."

She creamed her face clean and brushed her teeth, then crawled into bed after giving thanks for the day. All in all, it had been most satisfying. She plunged at once into a deep and dreamless sleep.

Chapter Six

Friday morning after devotions and breakfast, Emily took care of her messages. First, to respond to her father. He was usually up early, so she phoned him.

"Hi, Dad. Got your message. Would the first week in August be a good time for me to come up?"

"Emily! Good to hear your voice. That would be a fine time. I'll write you in. How are you liking summer vacation?"

"I'm loving it, but I did have a bad shock. A woman in AA was murdered, and I'm the one who found her."

He expressed dismay and wanted her to come up right away, get out of town. She'd known he would worry. Unlike her mother, he was an alarmist.

"I'll be all right, Dad. It was awful at the time, but I want to stay here for now in case the detectives have more questions. I'll let you know what happens, and I'll see you in August."

"If you're sure. I'll book you a room here, then."

"That would be great. Bye for now."

Now to respond to Marianne. She'd be at work, so Emily decided to email. She confirmed that she'd be at the meeting tonight and approved Marianne's dinner choice for Saturday. She was about to head out the door for her walk when the phone rang.

"Hello?"

"Emily, it's Ed. I'm glad I caught you in. Listen, I just found out that there's going to be a memorial service for Molly B. on Sunday afternoon. Would you like to go?"

"I would. When and where?"

"It's at the Church of the Lighted Window. I guess that was her church. I could pick you up around 1:30. The service is at 2:00. That is, if you'd like to go together."

"That would be good, Ed. Let me give you directions to my place."

As she hung up, Emily wondered if this counted as a date. She decided that it did. A somber date, to be sure, but a date nevertheless. Good thing she was going out with Marianne first. She could get some pointers.

Meanwhile, Luz Gutierrez and Fred Hansen were meeting to plan strategy. Fred handed Luz a copy of the *Pasadena Star News*.

"Here we are on the first page, below the fold. 'Police Baffled by Park Murder.'"

Luz skimmed the article.

"Well, it makes us out to be fools, but we can't release the progress we have made. At least we recovered the bat in the culvert. Results back from the lab?"

"It was definitely the weapon. Blood matches. No prints on the bat, though."

"And we're sure the battery occurred in the park, not elsewhere."

"ME is certain of that."

"Okay. Perp took a lot of risks. Anyone could have seen him abduct Brannigan, anyone could have seen him in the park. I take it no one of the park neighbors saw or heard anything?"

"Nothing there."

"So we've got two groups to focus on. There's the AA connection and the family connection. Are you still liking the husband?"

"It's possible. Seems the marriage was not as sunny as he claims. According to neighbors, there were arguments and several occasions when she stormed out, slamming the door. Seems to have been friction about her going out so often to meetings."

"Okay, stay with it. In the meantime, I think we should cover two bases. That meeting is tonight, and the service is Sunday. Do you want to take the meeting?"

DENISE B.

"Sure. I like coffee and cookies. The goal is to blend in, right?"

"That's it. Get the routine, find out who knew Brannigan would be coming that night. See who stays late and then tail the speaker. I'll cover the service Sunday."

Back home from her walk, Emily shelved Elizabeth George. She wished that Havers and Lynley were on the case of Molly B's killer. Havers, in particular, was a relentless detective. Still, the detectives who were on this case seemed good. She wished she had some more information for them. She wished she could help more. She figured that the killer must have heard Molly B. that Friday night, to know that bourbon had been her drink. That bourbon meant that the killer must have wanted it to appear that Molly had had a slip, had given in and drunk again. So whoever did it hated the fact that she'd triumphed over alcohol.

Why the brutal beating? She shuddered to remember the sight of Molly's body. On impulse, she dialed her sponsor Elaine.

"Well, Emily. I haven't heard from you in awhile. I was about to give up on you."

"I'm sorry, Elaine. I should have called you right after finding Molly. I know I've been remiss."

"I forgive you. I know you check in when you need to. And I figured you were getting help. So what's up?"

"I've been thinking about the beating Molly received. I can't get it out of my mind. It was so frenzied. Why would someone do that?"

"Abusers are strange ducks. Usually, they want to control the victim. Death may not have been the primary goal. Death may have been a side effect."

"You mean it was accidental?"

"I mean the main goal was to inflict as much damage as possible. The abuser usually flies into a rage and can't stop himself. Has finding Molly brought back memories of your own abuse?"

"Yes. When I was on the street, I never knew when the next attack would come. I just knew it was in my certain future."

"You were living in fear."

"Yes. When I walked away from being homeless and victimized, it was the happiest day of my life."

"You're a survivor. Do you feel guilty that you escaped and Molly did not?"

"I don't know about that. Maybe. Mainly, it brought the fear back."

"Well, take precautions. When you go out, go with a friend. And above all, don't go on twelve-step calls alone. That may be how the killer lured Molly."

"Good point. I was going to a meeting tonight. I'll call Marianne and see if she can pick me up."

"There you go."

It was a relief to talk with Elaine. She was so practical and commonsensical.

That evening, Emily dressed in white pants and a blue flowered shirt. When she heard a honk, she walked out to Marianne's car.

"Thanks for coming by. I was going to drive, but Elaine wants me to be extra careful."

"I think she's right. And it's not far to go, for me to pick you up. So who's speaking tonight, do you know?"

"Just that it will be a man. Ed says he alternates."

"I thought maybe you had an inside track," Emily teased.

"No, but we are going to the service together on Sunday."

"I told you he likes you. Nervous?"

"A little."

"Just be yourself. That's what he likes about you."

At the meeting, Emily marveled again at the size of the crowd. Would she really be able to speak in front of such a large group? Yes, she decided. She'd just focus on the faces of people she knew.

Standing at the coffee urn was a man who resembled Fred Hansen. As she approached, she saw that in fact, it was Detective Hansen.

"Hello. You're joining us tonight?"

He winked at her. "Research."

Glad he was on the job, she looked around and spotted Ed in a small group by the literature table. As she approached, he beamed at her.

"You really were good last night. I'm glad I went."

"It was nice having you there."

A chubby man with a red face and balding head came bustling up.

"Ed. Have you got the line-up for July?"

"Hey, Tom. I've got it right here. Speakers and contact info. We're all set."

"Good, good." Noticing Emily, he stuck out his hand.

"Tom Carney. Secretary. Got to stay on top of the job, you know. Meeting this size takes a lot of managing."

She suppressed a chuckle. "Emily Davies. Looks like you've got everything under control here."

"So far, so good. Thought maybe the killing would scare people off, but we've got a full house. Ghouls, eh?" He tapped the page Ed had given him. "Thanks for this. Good to meet you, Emily." He bustled off.

"He certainly takes the job seriously."

"Well, you know what they say about a little power. Where are you sitting?"

"Up front with Marianne."

"I'll be right behind you with the speaker. He just gave me a call. He's running late but promises to be here by the time he's scheduled to go on."

"What will you do if he doesn't make it?"

"Fill in for him. Let's hope he shows."

John Warrender appeared behind Ed. Ignoring Emily, he tapped Ed on the shoulder.

"Ed, I've got someone good for you. Name's Elizabeth. I heard her Wednesday night in Temple City. Dynamite share. Here. I got her number."

"Thanks, John. I'll give her a call. July is booked and August is filling. Emily here will be speaking in August."

John glared at Emily. "Remind me to be out sick that night." He turned on his heel and stomped off.

Ed lifted a quizzical eyebrow. "Bad blood?"

"I contradicted him at Mumblers. It must have hurt his feelings."

"Feelings? John? He just likes to be right. I'd say he's definitely holding a resentment. Good thing I've got your back tonight, literally."

Emily laughed.

The speaker did show, sliding in during the break just before he was due to go on. He was in the music industry, and he liked to namedrop. He gave blow by blow descriptions of parties with famous people, all getting loaded on drugs and alcohol. Emily wondered if Zack were here. He hated it when people mentioned drugs at an AA meeting. Finding the speaker to be arrogant, she let her attention drift. The speaker did, she noticed, hold the attention of the younger crowd, so that was good.

"Win some, lose some," commented Ed at the end of the meeting. "I'm going on to Conrad's. Want to come along?"

"No thanks. That's enough for me for one night."

He grinned. "You can only take so many of the rich and famous, eh? Don't blame you. Still, I feel responsible for the guy. So I'll see you Sunday."

"See you then."

Marianne dropped her off and she got ready for bed. She liked the way Ed seemed to know what she was thinking. He'd picked up on her boredom with the speaker and had guessed the reason why. Having heard her story, he knew all about her background, but she knew almost nothing about his. She'd try and remedy that on Sunday.

Saturday morning, Emily made her weekly trip to the South Pasadena Library to stock up on books for the week. She was pleased to find two new books in the rental section, a Joseph Wambaugh and a Robert Crais. As a bonus, there was an M.C. Beaton in the new books section. She checked them out, paying a dollar for the rentals. A good haul.

Back home, there was a new message on the machine.

"Professor Davies? This is James Nelson from your English 101. I just checked the grades online and I'm wondering if there was a mistake with my grade?" He gave his phone number.

Sighing, Emily retrieved the grade roster for the class in question. There it was, Nelson. He'd gotten a mix of A's and B's, she saw.

DENISE B.

Carefully, she recalculated the grade. Yes, it turned out to be a 3.5, a definite B+. She called.

"James, Emily Davies here. You had a question about your grade."

"Yes, I wondered if it shouldn't have been an A. I saved all my papers and I could fax them to you."

"There's no need for that. I have a record of your grades. Let me walk you through the math." Explaining that she worked with a four-point system, she showed him how she had arrived at the total.

"So it's a 3.5 and it would take a 4.0 to get an A?"

"Even a 3.75 for an A-."

"You don't round up?"

"No, James."

With a heavy sigh, he hung up. Reflecting that if he'd put as much effort into the class as he'd put into trying for a grade change, he'd have gotten an A, she pulled a cold diet soda from the fridge and headed out to the patio with her new Wambaugh. Maybe, by reading him, she'd find out more about how the police investigate murder. Maybe it would help her understand what the real life detectives were doing.

She discovered that he was a master at police procedure and that he also loved to show officers clowning around and using graveyard humor. She supposed it was a matter of self-protection in what had to be a grim job.

At 5:00, she headed out to Marianne's. Taking Oak Knoll up onto Lake, she was impressed anew by the big homes and lush lawns. Once at Marianne's, they'd walk to the pizza place. She arrived and rang the townhouse.

"She says she'll be right down, Emily."

"Okay, Alex."

Marianne wore dark brown slacks with a brown and white checked shirt, heels to match.

"I feel grubby next to you, in my jeans!"

"Don't be silly, you look cute. Let's go."

At Red Brick, they each ordered a small pizza, pepperoni for Marianne and sausage and peppers for Emily.

"Pizza here is so good, it reminds me of New York. So what's new with you?"

"Not too much. The cops have not been back to question me. I don't know if they're making progress or not. No one's been arrested; that's all I know. How about you?"

"I think Alex has started drinking again. I knew it was just a matter of time once he stopped going to meetings."

"Oh, Marianne! I'm so sorry to hear it. What happened?"

"Well, he came home from taking clients out, and when he kissed me I could smell liquor on his breath. I confronted him, and first he denied it, then he said he'd taken 'just a few sips.'"

"If he starts up again, will you split up?"

"Oh definitely. I'd have to move out. He has a reputation for drunken violence. I couldn't take the chance."

"Well, if you ever need to get out fast, you can always come to me. You know where I keep the extra key, just in case."

"Thanks. On a cheerier note, are you ready for your date with Ed?"

"As ready as I'll ever be, I guess. A memorial service isn't much of a date."

"Sure it is. Start slow and who knows, you can work up from there. I think he works a pretty good program. I know he sponsors a few guys. Since he's now asked you out, you could ask him to something, logically."

"That's a good idea, if I have the nerve. There's a French movie at the Laemmle I'd like to see."

"Go for it, I say."

From the restaurant they made their separate ways to their usual Saturday night meeting, "Life on Life's Terms." There was a good crowd of about forty people. The leader talked about getting sober through a recovery house, and then tossed out as a topic for discussion "Coping with Fear." The topic elicited, predictably enough, comment on Molly B.'s murder and how fear of having a slip was a positive kind of fear that kept people sober. Emily reflected that most people were taking the interpretation of Molly's death that the killer wanted them to take: Molly had drunk again and been beaten by a fellow drunk. She decided to keep quiet on her own views, however. She needed to clarify her hunch.

After the meeting, Emily invited Marianne over to her place. "Want to come over for some cocoa or a soda? I'm just a few blocks away."

"Maybe for a little while. There's nothing much to go home to. Alex will just be watching TV."

Given the lateness of the hour, Emily poured them caffeine-free diet sodas over ice and they took the drinks out to the patio. It was cool and pleasant; the crickets were chirping.

"When I talked with Elaine, she suggested that Molly might have been lured out of the parking lot by someone who claimed there was a 12-step call to make."

"Someone persuaded her they had to go out and rescue a drunk? At that hour? Seems a little farfetched."

"Maybe so. Somehow, though, she got spirited away from that parking lot."

"My bet is that she was abducted. So how did your visit with your mom go? Was she worried?"

"Not at all. It's my dad who's the worrier. He wanted me to fly up to San Francisco then and there."

"And will you?"

"I don't think so. I can't get over the feeling that I'm needed here."

"It's all those mysteries you read. You want to be the one who solves it."

"True, there's that. By the way, John Warrender has really turned against me."

"Can you do anything about it? Do you care?"

"It's just that I hate to leave a resentment simmering between us. I don't care for the guy, given his history, but I don't like to make enemies. What do you think? Do I owe him an amends for showing him up in front of everyone at Mumblers?"

"Ah. You hurt his pride."

"Exactly. He was trying to come across as Mr. Good Guy, and I painted him as a fool."

"Why not ask Elaine what you should do? Me, I'd say he deserved it."

"Well, maybe so. I'll give it more thought. Want some more soda?"

"No, I'd better get going. I promised to pick up the doughnuts for the War Memorial meeting tomorrow, and that means getting up early."

Once Marianne had gone, Emily got ready for bed. Read awhile? She wasn't in the mood. Call Elaine? Too late, really. She yawned. Good, fatigue was catching up with her. After setting the alarm for seven, she turned in.

Chapter Seven

At devotions the next morning, Emily added a prayer that she would be herself at the memorial service with Ed—her best self. Getting ready for church, she chose a short-sleeved black dress with black and white buttons down the front. She decided it was flattering, made her look slimmer.

She arrived at church early and stopped to listen to the praise band warming up. Jane was singing with her sweet smile, and catching her eye, Emily waved.

"Emily, don't distract the singers!" commanded the leader of the band.

"And don't feed the bears," she retorted, and headed into the Fellowship Hall. There a few people were gathered around the coffee urn before the service. She joined them and engaged in small talk. Katharine appeared to be ignoring her. Had her letter been offensive? She should probably have read it to Elaine before mailing it. "Restraint of tongue and pen," she reminded herself ruefully. Pastor Hendricks ducked in for some hot water and lemon to help him get through the sermon.

"Emily, I haven't talked with you since the murder in the park. How are you holding up? Any nightmares?"

"Well, one nightmare of sorts. I dreamed that abused women were all together, crying out for justice. It made me want to be a part of that justice."

"I can understand the impulse. Since you're the one who discovered her, you want to see it through. Jane and I have been praying every night for you and for the police on the case."

"Thank you. I really appreciate that."

"Come by if you need to talk. I'm in the office every day except Saturday."

"I may do that."

The pastor's message focused on Christ's resurrection and appearance to the disciples after his death. His point was how startled they were to see Him, even disbelieving. He encouraged the congregation to be alert to the presence of Christ in their own lives, to personal miracles. Emily took heart. Christ was her higher power, after all. She needed to be sensitive to his presence and guidance.

Back home, she made a light meal of cottage cheese and tomatoes and was ready by 1:30, when, promptly, Ed rang the bell. He wore a light-weight navy suit with a blue and navy tie.

"You look great, Ed. Very color coordinated."

"Thanks. I try. Ever the fashion plate, that's me. You look very nice yourself." He kissed her on the cheek. "Shall we?"

On the drive, Emily put into action her decision to learn more about Ed.

"What do you do, Ed, when you're not in meetings?"

"Life after meetings, right? Actually, I recently retired. I was an accountant and was able to retire last year at 65. These days I go to the gym and the pool, and I also listen to a lot of jazz. How about you? What do you do outside of AA?"

"I'm a voracious reader. Mysteries, mainly. And I love going to movies." *It's now or never.*

"Would you like to go with me to a movie? There's one called *Paris Je T'Aime* in Pasadena."

"Great idea. What's that, Paris I love you?"

"That's it."

"Ever been to Paris?"

"Several times. I do love it. I took French in high school and college and went over to France as an exchange student once."

DENISE B.

"Oh well then, you'll be able to follow the language. You can tell me if they mistranslate the subtitles. I always wonder what I'm missing with foreign films. So what day is good for you?"

"Say Wednesday at 4:00?"

"Perfect. We'll go out to dinner after the show. Sounds like fun. And here we are. Now to find parking."

The lot was full but Ed was able to find street parking a block away, and they walked into the church. It was packed. Emily recognized many faces from AA and spotted, in the distance, Luz Gutierrez, who nodded to her.

The program featured a picture of Molly on the cover, a color shot that showed her glowing red hair. She looked radiant. A good choice. Family filled the front two rows; she and Ed were able to find seats in the back.

The minister spoke of Molly's strong faith and encouraged the crowd not to lose their faith even as they mourned her violent and horrific death. One of Molly's daughters spoke of her mother's love of gardening and touched briefly on her deep involvement with AA. There was singing. Emily followed along, noticing the urn that was up at the front of the church.

After the service, they joined the line to offer sympathy to the family. There were, Emily noticed, two husbands, children, a grandchild, and parents. A lot of grief. Murmuring what were surely inadequate words of comfort, she met the family. Then she and Ed went into a hall where coffee, tea, small sandwiches, and cookies were being served. They spotted Tom Carney, secretary of the Friday night meeting, piling a plate with sandwiches. That explained the chubbiness. Emily supposed that his red face was the result of his drinking years.

"Ed, and—it's Emily, right? Sad day. Thought I'd better come and represent the meeting. Show of support, you know. I was surprised that there weren't speakers from AA taking part in the ceremony. Plenty of sober drunks here who could have done it."

"Mm," agreed Ed. "Must be that the family wanted it that way. If you like, we could do a special, separate AA service later."

"Good man. Good idea. Why don't you get on it right away. Excuse me...someone I've got to talk to."

This time Emily didn't bother to hide a chuckle. "He certainly likes to manage things."

"Yes, that's Tom. He was an executive for State Farm. Old habits die hard."

"I saw a detective earlier. Wonder what progress they're making on the case."

"Yes. I noticed her too. Guess it's true what they say, have a police presence in case the killer gives himself away."

"So Detective Gutierrez interviewed you too?"

"Right away. Molly had my card in her purse from when we set up her speaking engagement. The detective especially wanted to know how I'd come to choose her, you know, what the procedure was."

"I don't suppose she had much prior knowledge of AA procedure."

"No. Some cops do, of course. A lot of cops in recovery. But not her."

After half an hour at the reception, Ed drove Emily home, giving her another feather-light kiss on the lips.

"That feels good," she said boldly.

"To me, too. Have a good rest of the day, and I'll call you about the movie."

Suddenly, it felt like things were moving fast. She decided to give sponsor Elaine a call.

"I've started dating," she announced without preamble.

"Well, dear, you've given it eighteen years. I'd say you're ready. Is it anyone I know?"

"Ed McGowan. Retired, taller than I am, active in the program, cute. He asked me out and I turned around and asked him out back."

"Good for you. No need to be shy. A good relationship is, I believe, a gift from God. There's a feeling of elation that comes, and I wouldn't want you to miss out on that. Just remember that the best ones are built on friendship first. Don't copy your drinking days and hop into bed with him."

Emily laughed. "No danger of that. We barely kiss. Anyway, my pastor once led a prayer for purity for the single members of the church."

"I second that. Good luck with your next date. Anything else on your mind?"

Emily filled her in on her doubts regarding John Warrender. "Do I owe him an amends, do you think?"

"I think when you heard him speak about his violence, it triggered all the pain and anger you still feel from your own experience. Why not write about it and then follow your conscience."

"Just one more thing." Emily explained about the conflict with Katharine at church.

"So you suspect your letter was too harsh? Why not go out of your way to salvage the friendship. Make sure to show her you appreciate her good points."

Deciding to take Elaine's suggestion about John, Emily took out her journal. As she summarized what John had said at Mumblers, she realized what had irked her most was his notion that to make amends was to ask forgiveness from the woman he'd wronged. That seemed to put the burden back on the woman who had, after all, been hospitalized by him. Had she herself truly forgiven the men who'd been violent towards her? Probably not. It was a formidable task. She prayed for Christ's lead and recalled his teaching that we were to forgive our enemies. Well, if it was a command, she'd simply have to do it.

Since she'd already eaten at the memorial service, she just had a bowl of soup for dinner and then spent the evening with Wambaugh. Central to his story was a wise old sergeant who acted like a mother hen with her chicks, shepherding his officers and cagily assigning them partners. The book held her interest until bedtime when, thanking God for a sober day, she drifted easily into sleep.

Monday morning, Emily made her way to the Women's Step Study meeting and made the coffee without mishap. As usual, Irene arrived first and took out her embroidery.

"You're sure a dedicated craftswoman."

WIDE OPEN

"It really helps. When my brain goes all squirrely, having something to do with my hands calms me down. It's a good therapy. So I forgot to ask: how did the grading go?"

"It went. I think I was fair, so your prayer was answered. I was able to get all the grades in, so now I'm officially off for summer."

"Good, so you'll be able to stay for the step study portion of the meeting."

"Right. What step are we on this week?"

"I believe it's Step Two: 'Came to believe that a power greater than ourselves could restore us to sanity.'"

"Oh good, that's one of my favorites."

During the meeting that followed, Emily enjoyed gazing out the picture windows at the tall trees. The meeting room was an aerie in a green oasis. After the group had read Step Two, she raised her hand to share.

"Step Two has been very important to me. When I was new, I really clung to it, because I knew I was insane. My thoughts were scrambled with wet brain; I couldn't string a sentence together. When I heard this step, I latched onto the word 'could.' I didn't even need to believe that God 'would' restore me to sanity. Just accepting that He could, that it was within the realm of possibility, provided the help I needed. And today, I treasure my sanity above all else, because I didn't always have it."

Others spoke on what a return to sanity meant to them, agreeing that soundness of mind was to be much desired. Most viewed "insanity" as the belief that a drink would solve problems. The meeting passed quickly. It was over at noon. Emily wished she'd arranged to have lunch with someone after the meeting. Irene, she knew, had to leave right away to catch the bus. She decided to ask the secretary, Perla.

"I'd love to. I'm free all afternoon, don't have to work until tonight. Where do you want to go?"

"How about Senor Fish on Mission and Grand? I love their fish tacos."

"I'll meet you there."

DENISE B.

As she crunched down on flaky fish in a soft tortilla loaded with salsa and sour cream sauce, Emily listened to Perla's description of her job.

"I teach meditation techniques. Tonight I'm holding a seminar at my home, and sometimes I contract out to give seminars for businesses. You should come sometime. It's not expensive: $20 a session."

Reflecting that it could get expensive if one went every week, but that she could use help with her meditation practice, Emily said that it sounded very interesting and asked where Perla had trained.

"Oh, I've been doing it for years now and have experimented with various techniques. I did go to India to study for a while. In fact, I've been twice."

"That's amazing. So you're really committed."

"Oh, I am. You know, maybe you could help me. I've been thinking of doing a book about it. You're an English teacher. Maybe you could go over the manuscript with me."

Uncharitably, Emily wondered if she should mention that for editing manuscripts she charged $50 an hour. As if reading her mind, Perla murmured, "I'll pay you or something. That is, I'll think of something to even things out."

Certain that they'd be able to come up with a reciprocal arrangement, and looking forward to increasing her knowledge of meditation, Emily came up with a suggestion.

"What you could do is swing by Crossroads, the 12-step bookstore, and do some research. Find out what publishers deal with meditation books and write to them."

"What a great idea! Thanks."

After lunch, Emily immersed herself again in Wambaugh. She wondered how it was that she'd missed all his previous books. Probably because she tended to stick with female authors and female heroines. Time to branch out.

That evening, she emailed Marianne to tell her that Ed had accepted her invitation to go to a movie and to reiterate that she should feel free to come to the cottage whenever she needed to.

While she hoped Alex's relapse was a one-time thing, one never knew.

Monday night. Go on to Mumblers? No. She'd run into John Warrender, and she still hadn't decided how to end their feud. She didn't want to allow him to keep her away from a meeting, but she just wasn't ready. Instead, she'd have an early night.

Tuesday morning, as she settled in with coffee in the patio, she heard her landlady's voice.

"Emily! Could you help me with this tray?"

"Of course, Jean." She lifted the tray of tea things and carried it out to the table.

"Thanks. Today the arthritis is flaring up, but I do enjoy early morning tea outdoors. You don't mind if I join you?"

"I'm glad of the company. After all, we share the patio."

"Good. So what have you been up to? Still going to that church with the nice pastor?"

"Oh yes. Every Sunday."

"I was really impressed by him when I called him as one of your references. You're lucky you have someone you can admire. I was brought up Catholic, and ever since the scandal with priests molesting children and the church covering it up, I haven't been back."

"What a shame you feel you have to deprive yourself."

"Well, there's no getting around it. We were taught that the priests were Christ on Earth. Christ's representatives. When they failed, Christ failed too. That's how I look at it."

"Maybe it would help if you tried to focus on Christ within instead of Christ without."

"Maybe. What I've been thinking is going to one of those holy roller places. You know, lots of shouting and jumping and loud noise. Might pep me right up."

Emily laughed. "I can picture that, all right. Good luck with it."

Tuesday featured one of her favorite meetings, the San Marino Luncheon. It sounded fancy but the meals always came out of cans from Smart & Final. As she ate corned beef hash, she visited with

Barbara and Ian, a charming couple in their eighties who, both widowed, had recently married. She offered congratulations.

"Yep, we did it April 1. April Fools' Day. Because we're a couple of old fools."

The speaker didn't show, so after lunch the leader played round robin, calling on someone from the floor who then called on the next person. It provided a lively variety and Emily enjoyed it. The people at the meeting were mostly retirees who had been sober twenty/thirty years, and she felt she could bask in their wisdom.

Back home she realized she was tired and, since she was off work, could take a nap. She curled up on the bed with a light quilt and thought of her favorite soporific, a line from Woolf's *Mrs. Dalloway*. The husband comes into the living room with a quilt and pillow, saying "An hour's complete rest after luncheon." The line always made her feel protected and safe.

After napping, she checked her email. There was a message from her mother and one from Marianne. Her mother thanked her for coming up and asked her how the crime solving was going. Marianne's was brief: "Go get him, tiger!"

Feeling hungry again, she went into the kitchen to examine the contents of the fridge and cupboards. Nothing too inspiring. Then the phone rang.

"Hello?"

"Emily, it's Jane. What are you up to?"

"Hi, Jane. I'm debating the relative merits of a frozen dinner and a hot dog."

"Why not come over here? I just made a Chinese chicken salad, and there's loads here. Then if you're up to it, you and I could take a walk."

"Sounds like a great plan. I'll be right over."

She headed west on Mission, past the antique shops in Old Town, and made a right on Meridian. She was able to park right in front of the Hendricks' bungalow. Pastor Paul opened the door.

"Come on in, Emily. Jane's just getting ready to serve."

After saying grace, a charming practice Emily often forgot when she ate alone, Jane scooped up her salad onto plates. It was a specialty of hers, and it was delicious: tender chunks of white meat mixed in with shredded lettuce and a tangy dressing, crispy noodles on top.

"These noodles are wonderful. Did you make them?"

"Yes. They're fun to do. They puff up fast when they hit the hot oil."

"Delicious. So you must be off work now."

"Yep. Feels really good. The garden sure needed my attention."

After they'd eaten, Paul volunteered to do clean-up so that Jane and Emily could take off.

"I thought we might go to Lacey Park in San Marino. Shall we take one car? I'd be happy to drive."

"That would be good. I've been there, but I forget how to get there."

Heading east, Jane steered out of South Pasadena into adjacent San Marino, where the homes were larger and more ornate. After winding through a series of streets, she parked right outside the gates.

"Here we are. They close up at night, but I think we got here in time."

Sure enough, the scrolled black metal gate stood open. The women chose a path that would take them around the circumference of the park.

"Lush, isn't it?" Emily remarked. "So much green. When I was small, I'd go hiking with my dad, and he'd take us out into the dry, brown hills of southern California. I'd always ask him, 'Where's the green? Find us some green.'"

"Yes, it's sure different here. When Paul and I moved out here from the Midwest so that he could attend seminary, it was a big adjustment. I was used to rolling fields of green. It'll be good to get back there for vacation."

"When do you go?"

"Mid-July. Paul's lined up people to preach while we're away. So you must hear a lot of preaching, what with both church and AA. Isn't an AA talk like a sermon?"

"Similar. More of a testimonial. The basic outline is to tell what it was like in the drinking years, what happened—a spiritual awakening—and what it's like now."

"And you'd just heard the woman who was killed the night before you found her."

"Right. I hadn't known her before that. But the talks are so revealing that it felt as if I knew her. That's why it was such a shock."

"Are you over it?"

"Yes, but my desire for justice remains strong. I wish there were more I could do to help the police investigate."

"In Jackson Braun's Cat Who series, the Siamese cat always knows when the crime happens and who did it."

"I could sure use such a cat."

Deciding they'd had enough of a workout after what must have been two miles, the women drove back to the Hendricks'.

"Thanks so much for thinking of me, Jane. We'll have to do this again."

"Definitely. Good thing we've got all summer."

Emily drove home and then, feeling pleasantly tired, crawled into bed.

When Wednesday dawned, she awoke to a fluttery feeling and remembered that today was her date with Ed. She made coffee and took a mug along with her journal out to the patio. As she sipped, she wrote about her feelings.

"The key here is to go into it with no expectations. That way I won't set myself up to be disappointed. After all, I don't have to pretend to be someone I'm not. 'Just be yourself,' Marianne advised.

"Now today: get to a meeting. That way you'll be occupied and won't obsess over Ed."

After a breakfast of bran cereal with raisins, Emily took another mug of coffee into the living room where she settled into her armchair and picked up Wambaugh, who carried her through until it was time to head out for the meeting.

She'd chosen "Home at Last," a women's participation meeting, and the topic for discussion was change. Several women focused on "change" as it appeared in the Serenity Prayer: "the courage to change the things I can." She raised her hand and, when acknowledged, said, "I'm coming up on a big change in my life. I've just begun dating again after a long time of going it alone. Frankly, I'm at a loss here. I sure know that I don't want to repeat the mistakes of the past. I feel like a teenager again. Wish me luck!"

As the meeting broke up and they were putting their chairs away, different women approached to say, "Good luck to you." One, a young mother of four, said, "I wouldn't worry about mistakes in the past. You've broken the pattern by getting sober. Your higher power will see you through this experience. Have fun!"

Surprisingly, as she was getting ready, Emily found that she was not nervous. She dressed in light beige pants and top with a blue jacket and felt both comfortable and attractive. Ed arrived at 3:30.

"So we're going to the Laemmle, right? Up El Molino?"

"That's it. There's a parking lot on El Molino and Union and we can walk down to the theater from there."

"Sounds like a good plan."

Since they'd be eating later, they agreed to forego popcorn, and settled in to watch the movie. Emily was charmed by the pastiche of short love tales by well-known directors, 18 in all, all set in Paris. Her favorite was narrated in atrocious French by a woman mail carrier who was visiting Paris on her own, to practice her French. It was told as if the character were presenting an essay to her French class back home in Denver. At the end, the character realizes with both joy and sadness that she loves Paris and that Paris loves her back.

As the credits rolled, she turned to Ed. "Well, what did you think? Too romantic?"

"Oh, not at all. I really enjoyed it. All different kinds of love."

For dinner he insisted that they go to a French restaurant in Monrovia. Emily had heard of it but never eaten there. She ordered a veal dish and Ed went for a "demi-demi," steak and lobster, each with its own sauce.

"First time I've been to a French restaurant without the wine."

"Me, too."

"Did you drink a lot of wine when you lived in France?"

"Oh sure. The family served it with the midday and evening meals. Children drank it too, mixed with water. I've often thought how tough it must be for French alcoholics to get sober, what with the wine being such a big part of their culture."

"Mm. And yet they do it. Another miracle. Now tell me about your church. I know it's important to you from hearing your pitch last week."

"It's a conservative church, which is funny, because I'm not conservative. What I like about it is how the people really care about each other and get involved in each others' lives. I also like the focus on interpretation of the Bible. Then, the pastor has been really good to me through the years. About seven years ago I needed to be hospitalized, and I felt very alone and afraid. He came every day to see me."

"Sounds like a man who really knows his job. I was raised Catholic, and once I got sober I began returning to Mass. Have you noticed that there are a lot of priests and nuns in AA?"

"I have, and I've heard some of them speak. Wonderful stories."

"Yeah, I'd like to get one guy, Father Duncan, for Friday night. He's really funny."

"I'd love to hear him."

"Well, shall we?"

"Sure. Thanks a lot for dinner and for paying for the show too. I was planning to take you, since it was my idea."

"I'm old-fashioned. The guy is supposed to pay. If you want, you can cook for me sometime."

Emily laughed. "My cooking's pretty basic. But sure, if you'd like."

He walked her to her door and gave her another of his gentle kisses. Then he pressed a card into her hand.

"Here. I've got your number, and now you have mine. In case, you know, you want to talk sometime."

"Fine. Thanks again, Ed."

"Good night."

Emily felt as revved up as if they had drunk wine with dinner. Was she high on his kisses? She'd feared it was too forward to suggest a movie about love, but he had seemed to enjoy it. And now he'd invited her to call him. Maybe she would at that. She remembered her first boyfriend, how they used to talk on the phone for at least an hour every night. There was always plenty to say. Here she was, almost sixty, and getting romantically involved. Well, why not? Barbara got married at eighty-two. Easy, now. Let's not jump the gun. Still, it was with a smile on her face that she got ready for bed.

Chapter Eight

Emily was so engrossed with Wambaugh that she almost missed the Thursday meeting at Eddie Park. Startled to realize that it was nearly 11:00, she made the short drive in time to help with set up. This was her favorite location, a carriage house set in a small green park. She helped the small crew set up tables and chairs and got the literature out on the main table. She was pleased when Sue arrived to help slice and butter bread for lunch.

"Sue, how good to see you again!"

"Welcome back. I've missed you."

"What's for lunch today, anyone know?"

"I think Cheryl, a new lady, is bringing a main dish salad."

Working together, they got the room all ready for the meeting. Emily got an iced tea and her cigarettes and stepped out to the porch. Sue followed. They'd been friends about ten years and had in common, as well as their alcoholism, the fact that they were both bipolar.

"What's new, Emily?"

"I've begun dating again. We're in the really early stages. But I haven't said a word about being manic depressive and needing medication. I'm afraid to scare him off. What do you think? Should I tell him?"

"Well, eventually you'll want to. Hopefully, as he reveals more of himself then you can too. But I wouldn't be in any rush to tell him. Sometimes even AA people are prejudiced against it. I don't talk about it myself, except to you. The one time I tried, I got a big spiel about how I should be able to control it myself without medication. As if it were a matter of will power."

"Well, that's the thing: I'm afraid of prejudice."

"You'll know when the time's right to mention it. Then, if he rejects you, you'll know he wasn't worth it in the first place."

The food arrived just before 12:30, and it was delicious. As the group was finishing eating, in lurched Martha, a relative newcomer, with signs of distress painted on her face.

"I need a drink! So I came here instead."

"Good for you. Have a seat. What's the matter?"

"I lost my job yesterday. I get no support at home. My brother is dying, and I can't get back to Minnesota to see him. Then someone I really trusted turned on me. She said I didn't even belong in AA."

"What a fool. Don't believe her. There's still some lunch left; why don't you get a plate. I'll save your seat."

Soon Martha was surrounded by a sympathetic audience, and Emily was glad that the burden of listening did not fall to her alone. The man on her right leaned over and whispered, "I don't know what to say to her."

"You're fine," Emily whispered back. "She just needs people to be here."

The secretary got up to start the meeting, and began by thanking those who had come early to set up. "Many thanks to Mike, Al, and Sue." Emily felt a strong flash of resentment. What about her? She'd come early and done a lot of the work. Speak up now? No, just tell the secretary next week that she had joined the set-up crew. That would be the only way to get credit. She remembered reading that alcoholics were hyper-sensitive. And so am I, she realized.

The speaker was a young guy with three years sober. He was nervous to be up front, but nevertheless managed to do a good job as he told of wild parties, then having a child and needing to raise her on his own.

"Once I realized I was too drunk to get her into bed, and was even passing out while she was playing, I knew it was time to get help. Today, thanks to AA, I'm able to be the best father I can be."

Emily thanked him and then returned eagerly to Wambaugh and his tale of the Hollywood station of the LAPD.

Around 4:00, she realized that she was almost out of food and needed to get to the market. Von's was a short trip away. When she was new, before she could afford a car, she'd walked to Von's and walked back pulling a small shopping cart. Things sure do get easier, she reflected. She got a carton of diet soda, a box of cereal with raisins, bananas, cottage cheese, peaches, salad makings, and a stack of gourmet frozen dinners. She remembered Ed's suggestion that she cook him dinner. Well, fortunately they hadn't set anything up yet. She supposed that if she had to, she could make him a pork chop casserole or Swedish meatballs, two recipes she'd copied from her mother's file.

Once she'd put the food away, she decided to give Ed a call. She copied the information from his card—address, phone, cell, email—into her address book and tossed the card. Then, after taking several deep breaths, she dialed.

"Hello?"

"Hi Ed, it's Emily. Just wanted to thank you for yesterday. I had a really good time."

"That was fun, wasn't it? We'll have to get together again soon. Will I see you tomorrow night?"

"Yes, I was planning on it."

"Good. Something to look forward to. If you get there early, we can visit. I'm picking up the speaker this time, just to make sure she's safe. We'll probably get there around 7:15."

"Okay, I'll show up early too. I'll look forward to meeting the speaker. See you soon, then."

"Until tomorrow."

There, that hadn't gone too badly. She'd taken care of the etiquette involved. And, after talking with Sue, she'd decided there was no rush to letting him know she was bipolar. She'd let him take the lead in revelations. After all, there was still a lot she didn't know about him.

She mixed herself a salad and made an herb omelet for dinner. As she ate, she was struck by the thought, *This would sure go nicely with a big goblet of white wine.* Shocked by the urge, she remembered reading in the Big Book that sometimes there was just no defense against the first drink and that at such times, it was crucial to rely on one's higher power. "Dear God," she prayed, "please stand in the way between me and that glass of wine." The urge faded.

Cleaning up, she remembered hearing a woman speak on meditation as mindfulness, and how even something as simple as the dishes could be a form of meditating. She'd try it. Focusing carefully on the sudsy water, she carefully scrubbed and rinsed and found it soothing.

When she retired for the night, she reviewed the day. What went right? She'd gotten to a meeting and had used prayer to help her past the urge to drink. She'd allowed herself to be helped by Sue. She'd thanked Ed. What went wrong? She'd allowed a resentment to get the better of her at Eddie Park. Did she owe an amends there? Just to herself. If she really needed credit for a good deed, she needed to make sure the secretary knew what she'd done. Drowsy now, she slipped into sleep.

Friday morning promised a gorgeous day: sunny, blue skies, light breeze. After her walk, Emily took coffee, cigarettes, and book out to the back patio to savor the rest of the morning. After a few chapters, she felt the urge to write herself, so she went inside to retrieve her journal.

"It's been almost two weeks, and Molly B's killer is still at large. The thing is, he could be anywhere. The police need to locate someone who is filled with rage, someone who is good at hiding that fact. What could cause such rage? At base, I suppose it's a deep resentment against women, in particular against sober women. Is it someone who can't, himself, stay sober? Is it someone whose wife or girlfriend left him because she wanted to have a sober life and he couldn't? I hate to think it, but we may never know.

"Obviously, we need to find someone who is strong, clever, and sneaky. Also someone who is very lucky, or else he'd have been seen in the park. Question. Was Molly raped as well as beaten? The police have not released that information. Indeed, they haven't released any information. Should I call them and ask to be brought up to speed? Does finding the body convey privilege? Probably not."

DENISE B.

Feeling frustrated by a lack of progress, Emily ate lunch and returned to the book until it was time to get ready for the meeting. It was a balmy evening. She chose a sage green top and a black flowered long skirt, with touches of sage and rose. Friday night, and she wanted to make a good impression. She went outside to wait for Marianne, who arrived soon after.

"Thanks so much for coming to get me. Elaine, I think, is being over-protective."

"No, she's a good sponsor. She's just looking out for you. Better safe than sorry. So I haven't heard how your date went."

"We had fun. He did make some noise about having me cook for him."

"Tell him he can cook for you. Maybe he has hidden domestic talent."

"Maybe so. How's Alex doing?"

"I don't think he's been drinking again after that one time. He knows that if he does, I'm outta there. If that's what's motivating him, it's fine by me."

At the meeting, Marianne and Emily mixed and mingled. Emily remembered the early days, when she had been afraid of people. It was true, what the Promises said: "Fear of people…will leave us." AA gave a good training in social skills.

She was surprised to see John Warrender heading her way. Had he gotten over his grudge? He reached her and gave her a piercing blue gaze.

"So Ed tells me that you're going to be speaking here this summer."

"That's the plan, yeah."

"Will you talk about how you got beaten up when you were out there?"

The question made Emily uncomfortable. "I don't know. Sometimes I mention it; sometimes I leave it out. Why?"

"Because you might want to think about what was your part in it. That's what we do, right? Find our own part? Better do it, or else you'll come across as a pathetic victim."

"My part was the decision to stay with men who were violent, instead of getting the hell out of there," Emily bridled.

"Her part," said Ed, who had suddenly appeared, "was simply to be in the wrong place at the wrong time. That's all there was to it." Protectively, he circled her shoulders with his left arm.

"Sometimes women like it," countered John.

"Not this woman," said Ed. "And this one will say whatever she wants when she's up at the podium. If you heckle her, you'll answer to me."

"Who's heckling? I was just saying..." and John walked away.

"Sorry about that," murmured Ed.

"Not your fault. You have no control over what he says. Thanks for backing me up, though. I'm not used to someone looking out for me."

Ed grinned at her. "Could you get used to it?"

"I might."

"You came with Marianne, right? Why don't you join us after the meeting this time? I'm chauffeuring the speaker tonight and I think you'd enjoy meeting her."

"I'll check with Marianne, but it sounds good to me."

The speaker, Virginia F., was slight in stature and had a mop of wiry brown hair touched with gray. She was probably, Emily thought, in her forties. She spoke of how hard it had been for her to accept that she was gay. She'd finally hit the gay bar scene in Hollywood and found herself closing places down, then waiting for them to open up again in the morning. She came to once in her truck, nestled close to her dog, who was covered in vomit. She moved from person to person, never able to find stability.

Now sober fifteen years, she had a sober partner and together they were raising the partner's two children.

Emily joined in the applause and went to thank Virginia. "I really enjoyed hearing you. You paint a vivid picture. I'll talk with you more at the coffee shop after the meeting."

Conrad's was a popular AA hangout. They were good about splitting checks, and they didn't chase people away who were only having coffee. Emily and Marianne spotted their group at a big table at the back and joined them.

"So how old are your children, Virginia?"

"Five and seven. They're a handful. Right now, my partner Ellen is working and I am responsible for child care. It means a lot of carpooling. I sure never pictured myself as a suburban mom, but today I love it."

"Are they old enough for Scouts?"

"The older one is. The younger one can't wait. Everything her brother does, she wants to do too."

"Ah, a classic little sister."

"That's it."

"How about your partner? What does she do?"

"She runs a temp agency. It's a challenge, but it gives her regular hours and good vacations. This summer we're all headed up to Yosemite."

"You going to camp?"

"That's the plan. The kids are really excited about it."

Tom Carney finished off his hamburger. "Anyone for dessert?"

The group declined. Marianne turned to Emily.

"About ready to head out? I should probably get back to Alex."

"Sure, I'm ready. Pleasure to meet you, Virginia. Have fun in Yosemite."

Back home, Emily got ready for bed and, deciding she was not sleepy yet, returned to her book. Wambaugh certainly gave his cops some wild adventures. She remembered the time back in grad school when she'd almost completed her degree and she received a letter inviting her to apply to a new program in criminology. She'd declined, thinking instead that she'd follow the pattern, write and teach English. What if she'd taken that different path? Would she even now be solving crimes? For one thing, she'd be better equipped to bring to justice the killers of the women in her dream.

The confrontation with John Warrender tonight had disturbed her. If she had not escaped the violent men in her past, she too would probably be dead now, and crying out for justice in someone else's dream. Maybe Luz Gutierrez'.

Ed had come out of nowhere to stand up for her. He'd also asked if she could get used to his protection. Could she? Did she want it? Or would it be better for her to learn to stand up for herself? Deciding that it had, after all, felt good when he spoke up for her, she turned out the lights and climbed into bed.

Chapter Nine

Luz felt like she'd just gotten to sleep when the call came through. She squinted at the clock: 4:00 AM.

"Gutierrez."

"It's Fred. Better come out to Victory Park in Pasadena. We've got another one."

"Another park battery?"

"Affirmative."

"I'll be right there."

Grateful that she'd moved to Silver Lake and wouldn't have far to go, she pulled on the clothes she'd worn the night before, adding a warm sweater against the early morning chill. Victory Park: big place in East Pasadena. Their killer was branching out.

She found Fred at the northern edge of the park, standing on cement by a picnic table. The responding officers had already strung crime scene tape and set up a bright light that spotlighted a woman's sprawled body. From where she stood, Luz could see a pile of clothing neatly folded, with a purse set on top of the pile. The purse was on its side, its contents spilled out on the ground. Near the body was an empty bottle of tequila, lying on its side.

She crouched for a better view of the body. The face was untouched, but the naked form showed signs of extensive bruising. The arms and legs were at odd angles. Another vicious battery.

"ME been yet?"

"On his way."

"Just like the last one."

"Except for the purse. Last time, it was untouched. For that, we have to thank the guy who found her." Hansen gestured to the farthest table, where a young man who was clearly homeless sat shivering. Luz went over to him. Hansen followed.

"Bob here saw the lady, thought she was passed out. Spotted the tequila, finished it for her. Saw the purse, began to go through it for cash."

Bob looked up. Tears had streaked the grime on his face. "I just thought maybe she had some spare change she wouldn't mind giving me."

"Find anything?"

"A five and a twenty. I gave it back. I gave it back to him. Am I in trouble? Only, I don't want to go to jail."

"You won't be in any trouble if you just answer our questions. Did you touch the lady?"

"No. I thought she was passed out. I didn't want to bother her. I went to check, make sure she was really out. That's when I saw she was hurt. I got her phone out of her purse, and I called you. That was right, huh? To call you?"

"That was right, Bob. That was good. Did you see anyone else?"

"She was by herself. I didn't see nobody else. I looked, in case her old man was nearby and might hurt me too."

"Okay, Bob." She stepped aside and conferred with Fred.

"One theory on the Brannigan case was that the perp was a park bum. Do you think this guy is likely?"

"I tend to believe him. He's pretty incoherent."

"Anyone run him?"

"Yeah. He's got a few drunk in publics, gone to warrant."

"Well, at least we'll know where he is." She turned again to Bob.

"You're not in trouble for this, Bob, but you've got some tickets you didn't take care of. Also, we'll want to talk with you again. You'll need to go with an officer."

"Jail! I should of ran off like I first wanted to." Slumping, he went off with one of the responding officers.

DENISE B.

"Wish I could have put him in a shelter instead."

"Bob wouldn't stay put in a shelter. They cut 'em loose during the day. He'd just go off and get drunk and stay out there. This way, we'll be able to contact him."

"Right. So do we know who she is?"

"One Virginia Farraday. Contact information's in the purse. Also, I recognize her. I heard her story last night."

"When you went to that Friday meeting?"

"That's right. She was the main speaker. Just like before. Looks like someone is targeting the female speakers. They alternate man, woman. Last week's speaker was a man, and he was left alone."

"So we need to look hard at the people who are regulars at that group. This tends to get Brannigan's husband off the hook."

The ME finished his initial investigation and went to speak with them.

"I should be able to do the autopsy today. Probably late afternoon. Right now, I'd say she was killed here early this morning. Again, looks like the battery is what killed her. Consistent with a baseball bat."

"Thanks." Turning again to Hansen: "Well, for what it's worth, let's get a house to house of the neighbors. Park this size, we probably won't come up with anything, but it's worth a shot. Then we'll need a team to search the area for the weapon and any other evidence he might have left behind."

"The bottle is different this time. Last time it was bourbon. Best I can figure, he goes with what the victims' favorite drinks were."

"So we're looking for someone who goes to that meeting and pays close attention. What have you learned from attending? Anything jump out at you?"

"Two people know in advance who the speakers are going to be. The guy who books them and the guy who runs the meeting; they call him the secretary."

"So we'll need to re-interview them. How about notification?"

"Might be better coming from you. The partner is a woman living in Sierra Madre. Couple of kids involved."

WIDE OPEN

Luz sighed. "All right. I'll take it. Meet you back at the station in a few hours."

Meanwhile, Emily slept in. Upon awaking, she briefly considered going to the morning meeting in Grant Park, but decided against it. Since the corner store had closed, the meeting had no coffee. She brewed herself a pot, took her pills with juice, made raisin bread toast, and took her late breakfast out to the patio. There was still some shade, but it was going to be hotter today. She'd wear shorts.

She'd showered, dressed, and was once again lost in Wambaugh's world when the phone rang.

"Emily, it's Ed." His voice was tight, as if he were choking out the words.

"Hi, Ed. What's wrong?"

"I've been with the police. Virginia was killed last night."

Emily swayed. Thoughts of a camping trip to Yosemite flashed through her mind. "But how…you were going to take her home."

"I did. Took her straight back to Sierra Madre after Conrad's. The lights were on, so she figured her partner was up. Oh, Emily. I thought if I chauffeured her, she'd be safe."

"It's horrible news."

"They found her miles from home, in Victory Park. It's just like last time. Listen, you can't come speak at the meeting until this killer is caught. I'm canceling all the women I had lined up. We just can't take the risk."

"No, I can see that."

"I've got to go. Just wanted to fill you in. Listen, I'll see you soon."

"Bye. Thanks for calling. I know it wasn't easy."

Numbly, she returned to the armchair near the window where she had been sitting. She thought about Virginia and her story. How proud she'd been, to be entrusted with the main childcare for Ellen's kids. How happy she was, to have escaped the bar scene. And now she was gone. Emily felt the tears come and let them fall.

When she was cried out, she called her sponsor Elaine and filled her in.

DENISE B.

"That's very grim news. Now you're going to need to be doubly careful. Still think I was overreacting when I said to ride with someone to meetings?"

"No. You were right. But the weird thing is, Virginia got a ride home. Ed took her, and when he dropped her off she was safe. No one knows where these attacks are coming from."

"It sounds to me like the targets are strong female speakers. Women who have overcome a lot. And you fit the profile. I'd say no speaking anywhere until this killer is caught."

"I'd say you're right."

It was too hot to go for a walk, and too hot to nap. After lunch of cottage cheese and a cut up peach, she poured herself a large diet soda over ice and positioned herself so she could take full advantage of the fan. She tried to get her mind around the horror of two brutal slayings and couldn't. She envied Luz Gutierrez, who would be getting actively involved. No point calling; the detective would be too busy. When her own phone rang, it was Marianne.

"I just heard. People showed up for a meeting in Victory Park and found scene of crime tape everywhere. It's an AA crime wave! I haven't been this upset since that time years ago when a guy with longtime sobriety killed his ex-girlfriend, her kids, and himself. That was shocking but at least everyone knew who did it."

"Well, that's the thing. We don't have a clue. Pretty soon, everyone is going to look suspicious. So now what. I was trying to decide whether or not to go to the Saturday night meeting."

"Life on Life's Terms?"

"Yeah. I don't want to let these killings keep me indoors cowering."

"Okay, let's do it. Shall I pick you up? You're on my way."

"If you wouldn't mind. Elaine was really firm on the buddy system."

"Got it."

The heat and the horrific news had taken her appetite away, but she felt she should eat something so fixed a small salad for dinner.

Was it wise to go to the meeting? Undoubtedly, the talk would center on Virginia. But better to be with other people than to mourn alone. She and Marianne easily found space in the parking lot of the church and walked up to a cluster of people outside the door.

"Emily! I hear the cops want to shut down the Friday meeting. Can they do that?"

"Is it true she was drunk on tequila? I heard they're holding a homeless guy who was drinking with her."

"How could a homeless guy afford tequila?"

"Maybe she bought it. And then went looking for a lower companion and found the killer."

"No. It's someone at that Friday night meeting. I wonder if any meeting is safe now."

"This is supposed to be the safest place for us. If this gets taken away, what do we do?"

The ten-minute speaker had known both Virginia and her partner Ellen. She spoke of their life together, how happy they were and how well-suited. She opened up discussion on how to remain sober while mourning.

Emily decided to share her dream vision of women who had been battered and who were crying out for justice. "That may sound far-fetched, but I believe it's true. I'm hoping that justice will come soon. As to how to stay sober? We need to remember that both Molly and Virginia went out of their way to tell their stories in order to help others. That's nearly the last thing they did. By remaining sober, we honor them."

Once Marianne had dropped her back off at home, she realized she was scared. Knowing it was unlikely that someone would sneak in and murder her in her bed, she nevertheless double-checked the locks on all the doors and windows. After fervent prayer that the fear would lift and the killer be caught, she went shakily to bed.

Sunday morning, she got ready for church and looked forward to seeing the Hendricks. She'd phoned them the previous day once she'd gotten the news. Pastor Paul led prayer, focusing on the urgent need to stop the killer. Jane came up to her and hugged her after the service.

"Emily, how terrifying for you. Have you thought about keeping away from AA meetings until this is resolved?"

"No, I haven't. It's such a big part of my life."

"But it isn't safe now. Could you just have informal meetings, get-togethers with friends you trust?"

"That's a thought. And I really appreciate your concern."

As usual, when told not to do something, Emily went right ahead and did it anyway. From church she headed up the road to the War Memorial meeting, intending just to stay until break. She got coffee and a few pieces of doughnut and looked for Marianne, who was a regular there. She spotted her outside on a bench, having a cigarette and talking with a tall woman sporting horned rim glasses and wearing a linen suit.

"Emily, hi. This is Donna. She was scheduled to speak on a Friday night in July."

"Hey, Donna. I'm sorry we'll have to miss your story."

"Well, I'm sorry too, but it's obvious we can't take the risk. Hopefully the cops will catch this guy soon and we can all get back on track."

"Donna and I were talking about getting Peter on the case."

"Peter?"

"You've met him. He used to come to this meeting all the time. He's a private investigator. We figure his being already in AA and knowing lots of members might give him an edge."

"Who would actually hire him?"

"We hadn't gotten that far. The families? A group of us in AA all making a contribution?"

"Well, it's worth considering, at least."

The ten-minute speaker told of running his own advertising agency and the heavy drinking involved, all excused as "entertaining clients." He'd come to AA on a court card, and his original intention had been to go along with it and, in the process, to prove AA wrong. Instead, he'd gotten sober. At the end, he tried for a joke about speakers being bumped off. "I figure I don't have to worry, because I'm the wrong sex." Predictably, the joke fell flat.

Emily slipped away at break. After fixing herself another lunch of cottage cheese and peaches, she took her journal to the armchair and settled in.

"Jane has a point about staying away from meetings. I'll keep attending my regular ones, but I will boycott Friday night. Let Detective Hansen and/or Peter investigate that one. Now, where is the killer hiding? Whom have I met since going to Friday night?

"There's a large crowd from the local recovery houses. They're just getting sober and might resent the process. But they're out, because the van picks them up right after the meeting and takes them back to the house.

"There's John Warrender. I wouldn't want to be alone with him. He's held a resentment against me ever since I corrected him at Mumblers. He has a history of violence, and he's certainly strong enough. He's a possible.

"There's Tom Carney. Every month, he gets a list of the speakers from Ed. He's very controlling, needs to be in charge. Elaine said that the killer was probably a control freak. But he's heavyset and out of shape. Would he be strong enough?

"I hate to say it, but there's Ed. He's traveled far and wide to find both male and female speakers, so he's familiar with their stories. He works out, so he's strong enough. But I have no idea what his motive would be. Having speakers killed off reflects poorly on him. Besides, he chauffeured Virginia Friday night and when he dropped her off, she was fine.

"Could it be a woman, someone who's jealous of other women with long lengths of sobriety? She'd have to listen closely, buy the right bottles, make her move. Can't rule that out.

"Then there's the unknown assailant. There's where we run into trouble. He or she could be in any one of those 300 chairs, watching and waiting, planning and scheming, and appearing to be totally innocent."

Emily set the journal aside. She hadn't solved it, but she'd been able to clarify her thinking. That, at least, was worthwhile. Now what? She didn't feel like reading, she didn't like daytime TV, she'd already eaten. She decided to take a walk.

Staying on the shady side of the street, she moved through the neighborhoods of South Pasadena. She passed people out on bikes, people pushing strollers, people with dogs. Most smiled or waved. It

DENISE B.

restored her to normalcy. She walked quite a ways, returning home around 4:00. Pleasantly tired, she took a diet soda out to the patio, where there was a breeze and where she could watch her hummingbird feeder.

She practiced deep breathing like Perla had suggested and let herself slide into a meditative trance. She was in a meadow filled with wildflowers, looking up at the blue sky. She was surrounded by the presence of God. In the distance, she saw two figures coming. They were Molly and Virginia, restored to beauty, lithe and strong.

"Don't keep us in the victims' room," they said. "You are very near a solution." She wanted to engage them in conversation, but they mounted a silver horse and rode off into the distant hills.

Slowly, Emily opened her eyes. She felt very peaceful. She understood that Molly and Virginia wanted to be remembered as strong and victorious, not as victims. Near a solution. She hoped so. She really hoped so.

It had been quite a day. Now the sun was setting; the sky was a mass of color. Before she had dinner, she would call Luz Gutierrez. Up until now, she had held back, afraid to get involved and to impinge upon the investigation. But some things needed saying.

Luz was unavailable, but Emily left a message for her to call. She hoped that when the time came she'd have the courage to make her suggestion. Of course, she was only a civilian. But she finally had an idea.

Chapter Ten

Monday morning, Emily got ready to head up to Neighborhood Church to make the coffee for the Women's Step Study meeting. Once there, she was delighted to discover that once again the custodian had been already and had set up the chairs in neat rows and filled the coffeepots. This was certainly easier than the olden days at the meeting's original location, when all set-up chores were left for the members to do.

She'd just gotten the coffee perking and the tea water heating when, to her surprise, Sue arrived.

"Sue, how great to see you!"

"I've been wandering around the grounds, looking for the meeting. I finally met up with the church secretary, who directed me here. I saw your car in the lot, but I didn't know where I was going."

"I'm so glad you found it. Coffee will be awhile, but I put out a little pot for hot water if you want to make a cup of instant decaf."

"Thanks, I will."

"So what brings you here today? You don't usually come."

"Just thought it would be a good idea to make it to more meetings."

"Wonderful idea. I think we'll be reading Step Three today."

"That'll work out perfectly. My sponsor has had me read Steps One and Two on my own, and I just finished."

"Couldn't be better."

DENISE B.

"How about you, Emily? Have you told this guy you're dating about being bi-polar?"

"Not a word. I figure, why does he have to know? If we were getting married, of course I'd fill him in, but we're just in the early stages."

"I don't tell anyone, myself. Not after I mentioned it at the Tuesday Luncheon meeting and Lenore gave me a big lecture on will power and how the meds could be breaking my sobriety."

"Yeah, there's a lot of misunderstanding out there."

Others arrived, and before too long the room was full. The leader spoke of losing a young child, and how the pain of it had driven her to drink, and how recovery then improved her relationship with her remaining children. After break, everyone took a turn reading a paragraph of Step Three: "Made a decision to turn our will and our lives over to the care of God as we understood Him."

Discussion was lively. Most people agreed that the proviso "as we understood Him" was crucial to their faith. A surprising number had been raised with a punishing God and had been able to redefine God as a being of Love. Emily told how, when she was new, she'd been much helped by a nun at an AA retreat. The sister had told her that really God was neither male nor female, but Spirit. But her God knew that it was easier for her to call God "She," so she did, and was stronger in her faith because of it. Emily was much helped by the permission to change pronouns, since she had been editing her copy of the Big Book and changing every "he" to a "she."

Another woman raised her hand and was called on. "I'm having a lot of trouble believing in any god since these murders. The women who were killed had a lot of sobriety, and I'm sure they had worked Step Three. They'd gone ahead and given their will and their lives to God. And what happens? God allows them to be beaten to death. What kind of cruel god does that? To me right now, divinity is just a big mean joke."

Emily wished she had an answer for her. It was an age-old roadblock to faith, the question of how God could allow injustice in the world. She hoped the woman wouldn't give up entirely.

WIDE OPEN

The meeting ended at noon, lunchtime. Emily and Sue decided to go out to eat and, at Sue's suggestion, drove to La Fiesta Grande on Mission. The place was packed but they were able to get a booth.

"Guacamole to share?"

"Sure, why not."

Sue ordered fajitas and Emily a crispy beef taco.

"I'm glad I went to the meeting. People really jump in and share, don't they?"

"Yep. It gets pretty lively. You kept quiet, though."

"I have a lot of trouble sharing at meetings. I do fine one on one with someone I know, like you. But I don't like to risk baring my soul to the whole room. That's just something I need to work on, I guess."

"Maybe if you come every Monday and get to know the women, it will get less intimidating."

"You're probably right."

Emily was only a short distance from home. When she got back, the mail had arrived. There was a letter from the IRS. Surely she'd paid her taxes on time this year? With trepidation, she opened it. Enclosed was a check for $425 and a notice telling her that she had miscalculated the amount due on her return. This refund was the balance.

What a lovely surprise. Bonus money. She could go out to dinner at Shiro or the Arroyo Chop House. Whom to invite? She'd have to think about it.

Emily walked to the bank to deposit the check, and on the way home stopped off at Rite Aid for facial cleanser, Q-tips, calcium, and a new lipstick. She tended to let the necessities pile up so that she could take care of them all in one fell swoop.

Once home again, she knew it was time to make a call she'd been putting off.

"Hello, Ed?"

"Emily. How's the day going?"

"Oh, I'm enjoying it. The reason I called: last time we went out you said I couldn't pay but I could invite you over for dinner. My repertoire is small, but I can put something together, and I wondered if you'd like to come over sometime this week."

"That would be great. I can do it any night but Friday. I have to salvage what I can of the Speaker Meeting."

"How about Wednesday around 6:00?"

"Perfect. I'll be there. Thanks for asking. And don't worry about its being gourmet. I'm easy."

"Okay, I'll keep it simple. See you soon."

There, that was set. Everything was going according to plan. She hoped that meant she was following God's will for her life. Time for a short nap and dinner. Then there was one more task she couldn't put off. To do it, she'd have to make Mumblers. When the time came, she made the short trip to Oneonta Church and headed for Button Hall.

She was early; the meeting started at 8:00 and it was only 7:30. But she needed to be ready to pounce. She got some coffee and stationed herself outside the door with a cigarette. She spotted her prey sauntering down the walkway.

"John, do you have a moment?"

He paused and looked at her suspiciously with those fierce blue eyes. She took a deep breath.

"I owe you an amends for the last time I was here. You revealed something from your past and shared from the heart about it. I took it personally and corrected you with cross-talk. I shouldn't have done that, and I apologize."

"No. You shouldn't have done it," he muttered. "I need some coffee. Excuse me." He walked away.

Well, they'd never be friends. But had least she'd done what she needed to, taken care of her part in the feud. Now maybe they could just ignore each other. Not every amends had a blissfully happy ending.

"...And when we were wrong, promptly admitted it." Yes, she'd thought John's apology to the ex-wife he had hospitalized was too weak and namby pamby. But in her rebuttal she'd essentially put him down in front of the whole group. She'd been in the wrong there. As for prompt, well, it had taken her two weeks. But she'd gotten there.

Emily flashed to her journal and list of suspects. Had she just made an amends to a killer? If so, so. At least now her conscience was clear.

She found a seat and tried to focus on the meeting. Put a question in the hat? Why not. She'd borrow the concern that had arisen at this morning's meeting: "How do you reconcile the idea of a just God with these killings?"

Question and answer time. "How do you fire a sponsor? Is it okay to do?" The general consensus was that if the sponsor was chronically unavailable, it was fine to let him or her know that another sponsor was needed. One man bragged that he'd never needed a sponsor since he just used the group. Emily quelled the impulse to correct him. One amends was enough for one night.

Her question was unfolded and read to the group. Answers varied. "It's not God who is to blame here but a specific evil person. It's true that good and evil exist. It's up to us to choose the good, which we do when we get sober." That one was her favorite.

Back home, Emily saw she had only a chapter left in Wambaugh, so she settled into her armchair to finish. His main thesis, illustrated by many short adventures, was that good police work was fun. She hoped so. She really hoped that Luz Gutierrez and Fred Hansen were having fun.

Tuesday morning her cleaning lady arrived. She'd met Rita in AA. Rita had told her she was starting her own cleaning service and was looking for clients. Since she only charged $15 an hour, they'd struck a deal. Rita now had enough work that she could indulge in her passion, sailing. She didn't have her own boat, but she was welcome as a crew member at the marina.

Emily liked to leave Rita alone to do the job, so she packed up her journal, a new M.C. Beaton, and a diet soda and headed for Garfield Park. It was the first time she'd been back to the park after the chilling discovery of Molly's body. She avoided the overgrown area where Molly's fallen form had lain and settled in under a large oak at the southern end of the park.

She reviewed her list of suspects and let her thoughts flow freely. Then she turned to Beaton and her Hamish Macbeth, who preferred a simple life in a village in Scotland to a promotion and move to the big city. He always solved the crime, which was very satisfying. In her meditation, Molly and Virginia had told her she was very near a solution. That, she would hold onto.

Her cottage, when she returned, gleamed, and Rita had left her a small bag of homegrown tomatoes. She'd use them in a salad, and the place was now in excellent shape for tomorrow night. She hoped she'd be ready as well.

Emily checked the clock. If she left now, she could make the Tuesday Luncheon meeting and talk with Barbara. Sure enough, she made it. There was even a parking space in the shade, so the steering wheel would not be too hot to touch when it was time to leave.

She got herself a cup of iced tea and first went up to Norma.

"I want to thank you for including me in your prayers. You said you'd pray that I found enough work for fall semester. Well, it worked. I've got five classes lined up."

"That's wonderful! I'm glad it helped."

The newlyweds arrived. Barbara hugged her and asked if she'd like to step outside, their code for having a cigarette. If Barbara, in her eighties, was still smoking with no ill effects, Emily figured there was hope for her. Taking their drinks, they walked around to the designated smoking area at the back of the building.

"Is there any news on your book?"

Years before, Emily had written up her experience as a homeless woman. A publisher had expressed interest, requested changes, and then remained silent.

"Not a word."

"I can't understand it. It's such a good story. Is it possible to show the book to somebody else?"

"Oh, sure. But I tried an agent who sent it around to the big houses, and they liked it but weren't interested. With the small presses, there's one who liked it and wanted to publish it. They even sent me a contract. But right about then was the time I went off my medication, got manic, and had to be hospitalized. When the publisher found out, she cancelled. She needed me to be in good shape to promote the book. She wanted, you see, a real success story.

"What I've been thinking about is writing her again, telling her I made a full recovery and am now back teaching, and asking her for a second chance."

"It's certainly worth a try. She could say yes."

"Well, I've been putting it off."

"It's summer vacation now and you've got the time. Just do it." Barbara fixed her with a look of determination and command. It was probably a look she'd used on her children when they were small.

"Okay, you're right. I'll do it." Emily was cringing inside, but now she'd made a commitment to Barbara and she'd made the same one to Irene, who also wanted to see the book published. That was the thing with AA. People wanted you to follow your dreams and to do everything possible to make that happen. They wouldn't put up with excuses.

They dined on chili and salad and settled in to listen to the speaker. He spent very little time on his experience drinking and instead put the focus on recovery. He worked in the field and spent a lot of time counseling newly sober people, telling them he'd do his best for them, but that they were not to put their trust in him. "I'm just human, and humans will let you down. You need to put your trust in God."

He'd recently joined a gospel church and was a deacon. He loved it but felt that AA remained his main religion. Church helped him maintain a conscious contact with God, but AA was everywhere and not limited to one building.

The shade had worked, and Emily was comfortable driving home. Hopefully, she checked the mail, but today there was no pleasant surprise like a contract from the publisher or yesterday's unexpected check. Just junk mail. Maybe there would be something on email? She logged on. Nope. Just SPAM. Well, she'd send a message to Marianne.

"We on for Saturday night? I believe it's my turn to choose. Probably Brits again, if you don't mind the repetition. Tomorrow night Ed is coming over for dinner. Wish me luck!"

Might as well shop for tomorrow. Chops, rice, onion, bell pepper, salad stuff. And she already had tomatoes. She'd put one in the salad

DENISE B.

and one in the casserole. The recipe was easy: brown the pork chops. Put six tablespoons raw rice in a casserole dish. Set chops on top, and cover each chop with a slice of onion, pepper, and tomato. Salt and pepper. Sprinkle marjoram and thyme. Pour in a can of beef broth, cover, and bake at 350 for one hour. The rice would get all fluffy and flavorful, as juice from the vegetables mingled in. And hopefully the chops would be tender too.

So, tomorrow she'd get domestic. For tonight, it was microwave a frozen dinner. She'd eaten and done the dishes and was about to settle in with Beaton when the phone rang.

"Hello?"

"And just when were you going to tell me about the second murder?"

"Hello to you too, Dad."

"Honestly, Emily. I had to hear about it from an old friend in Villa Gardens. You didn't think I needed to know? Didn't want to worry me, I suppose you'll say."

"Well, there is that."

"I think you should come up for a visit now. Forget August. Anything could happen between now and then. It's obvious to me that you need to leave town. I know your summer plan of a meeting a day, but any meeting could be your last."

"I've spoken with the police in charge. They're very near a resolution."

"So all power to them. You don't have to stick around to see it. You can be safe up here, and my friend can call if the thing gets solved. Come on, don't be stubborn."

"Let me think about it."

"Don't think too hard. United has a nice cheap flight up to San Francisco on the shuttle right now."

"I'll let you know in a couple of days."

"No more than a couple. Meanwhile, I hope you aren't going to any meetings alone."

"I won't from now on."

"Promise."

"I promise. I'll talk with you soon. Good night, now."

That was the second time today she had given her word. Well, she intended to keep it. She relaxed into Beaton's world, wishing for Hamish's acumen, and was startled when 10:30 rolled around. She was really on a summer schedule now, what with no classes to get up early for. Brush and floss teeth, cleanse and cream face—her beauty regimen. Thanking God for a sober day, she climbed into bed with a sense of satisfaction.

Chapter Eleven

Laura checked her watch again. 11:00! She'd given Josh a 10:00 curfew and had hurried home from the meeting so as to be home when he arrived. At sixteen, he was just getting too wild. There was, of course, no father to guide him, but the marriage had never been any good and she'd been divorced since the boy was five.

She should never have let him go out tonight. School night. He'd said it was a study session with friends. Chemistry. Brain chemistry, more like it. Well, she'd ask her steady boyfriend for his advice. He'd never raised a son, but he was male, wasn't he? Maybe he could provide some insight.

The phone rang. Was it Josh, stranded? Willing herself to be calm, she lifted the receiver.

"Josh?"

"No, honey, it's me. He's not home yet?"

"Hi, you. I was just thinking about you. No, he's not home, and I don't know what to do about it except confront him. He'll just mumble some excuse, I know."

"Want me to have a chat with him?"

"Would you?"

"Sure. No promises, but I'll give it a try. Listen, the reason I called is that I just got contacted by Central Office. You know how I've got my name on the list for 12-step work."

"And you have to go out on a call?"

"I said I'd do it. It's a woman, only eight days sober, who found herself at a bar. At the last minute, instead of ordering a drink, she called AA. So it's rather urgent I get there quickly. What I wondered: would you come with me? Give it the woman's touch?"

Laura hesitated. "I really wanted to be here for Josh, honey."

"Hate to say it, but he wasn't there for you. Leave him a note. Show him you're going to go ahead with your own life instead of obsessing over him. Then this weekend, I'll talk with him."

"Well, I suppose I could. I'm still in the AA groove from speaking tonight."

"And you were wonderful. That's why I thought of you at once."

"Okay, sure, I'll do it. Do you want to pick me up?"

"I'll be there in fifteen minutes."

Glad she hadn't gotten into her pajamas yet and that she'd drunk plenty of coffee during the meeting, Laura quickly re-applied lipstick and brushed her glossy black hair. She then scribbled a quick note for Josh, leaving it prominently displayed on the kitchen table. If she knew her son, when he came home he'd head straight for the kitchen. "Had to go out on an AA call. Be back as soon as I can. We'll talk in the morning—Mom."

The doorbell rang.

"Hello, dear. That didn't take long."

"I wasn't far away. You look gorgeous, by the way. It will be good for this shaky woman to see such a lovely model of sobriety."

"Well, thanks. I'm still dressed up from my speaking engagement. So how far away is this bar?"

"It's the Thirty-Fiver on Colorado in Pasadena. Ever drink there?"

"Probably. I think I hit every bar in the San Gabriel Valley. Do you think we'll get there in time?"

"Hope so. At least she had the good sense to call AA. She said she'd be waiting out front. We should leave now, honey."

They headed for the car, Laura walking in front. Suddenly she felt a tremendous pressure on her throat. No, it couldn't be happening! But it was, and she went limp.

DENISE B.

When she came to, very groggy, she was flat on her back in wet grass, swallowing convulsively. Vodka? She tried to spit it out, and the pressure returned.

"Josh!" she screamed silently. It was her last conscious thought.

Her body was not discovered until 8:30 Wednesday morning, when the gardener made his rounds with a leaf blower. Luz and Fred, en route to work in the City of Commerce, turned around and made it back to Grant Park, Pasadena.

"Clothes in a neat pile, purse undisturbed on top. He wants us to identify the bodies."

"This one was beaten, like the others, but not as severely."

"The ME speculates that this time, the killer went overboard with a choke hold and it was that that killed her. Or maybe he was interrupted."

"If so, that'll mean witnesses. Canvas is going on as we speak. Maybe we'll get lucky this time. There are several small houses around. Seems to be a neighborhood park."

"I'm glad it wasn't kids that found her, on their way to the swing set."

"This time the baseball bat is obvious, right in plain sight. Like he's mocking us."

"Might be worth it to check with sporting goods stores, on the off chance he's buying them in bulk."

"Oh, definitely."

"Well, we have to talk with the lieutenant. For one thing, I need to ask him about what Emily Davies had to say. She was quite definite."

"I'll take care of notification, then. You go ahead. We can rendezvous later this afternoon."

By then, the detectives had learned that Laura Miller was a divorced mother with a sixteen-year-old son. She'd worked as a loan officer at a local bank. They also had found out that she'd been the main speaker at a Tuesday night meeting.

"So the Friday night meeting is closed off to women speakers, but that doesn't stop him. He just spreads out to a different meeting."

"There are how many meetings in the area? Hundreds? Thousands? He's got a non-stop supply of victims. Realistically, we can't stop them all from getting women speakers."

"Time to move on Plan B?"

"I'd say so. It's worth a try."

"It's unorthodox, but it just might work."

Chapter Twelve

Wednesday, her big day, had dawned. Emily had devotions out on the patio; it felt like it was going to be another beautiful day. She planned it out: get to the Women's Discussion meeting; prepare casserole; get herself ready; entertain. Didn't sound too arduous. She prayed for the strength to see it through.

As she drove into the church parking lot, she was amused by the big red banner out front: "God is still speaking! Never place a period where God has placed a comma." She mused, as she did each time she passed the sign, that if God were placing a comma where a period could go, then God was guilty of the punctuation error known as a comma splice. Understandable, she supposed. After all, it often confused her students. Two independent clauses cannot be joined by a comma alone. The way to join them is either with a semicolon or a comma along with a coordinating conjunction.

She got to the meeting early and was pleased to see that the coffee was ready and the refreshments already set out. Cheese, crackers, and fruit: a good light lunch. She'd made a commitment not to walk around the building and smoke at this meeting, but to stay and socialize instead. It was, she felt, too isolating to leave for a cigarette before the meeting and after break.

It was amazing how many women were available between 1:00 and 2:30 on a Wednesday afternoon. Some, of course, were retired. Others were young stay-at-home moms who brought their little ones along. The rest seemed to be able to take a long break in the middle of the day. Either they had flexible hours or they worked for themselves.

Irene was there, having set up all the chairs by herself. She'd done a very neat job.

"Come sit over here by me," she suggested, fingers flying with a crocheting project. "I want to thank you for praying about my beautician's license. It finally arrived. Now, I don't want to work, but if I have to so that we can get by, I will."

"I'm glad it arrived."

The ten-minute speaker talked about what a struggle it had been for her to get sober. It had taken her ten years to do it, racking up a year here and two years there but always slipping until finally, it took.

She chose as the topic of discussion "Terminal Uniqueness." Most of the women believed that, in their drinking days, they had wanted to be very unique and special, set apart from and superior to others, and that after coming into AA, they learned to focus on what they had in common with other women.

One woman looked very distraught and kept waving her hand, hoping to be called on. But the meeting was cut short by elections for the next term's officers, and she never got a chance. Emily hoped that she'd be able to stay after and talk with her sponsor, who was also present.

The meeting ended, and as they carried their chairs into the back room to stack them, Emily mentioned to Irene that she was entertaining a gentleman caller that evening.

"I'm actually quite nervous about it."

"I'll be praying for you. Maybe you won't be a bachelorette much longer."

As everyone began to head for the parking lot, the woman who'd been the speaker grabbed a gavel and began pounding it on the table.

"Listen up! I just heard on my cell phone, there's been another murder. She was found in Grant Park this morning."

She was surrounded by women with questions and excited responses. Disbelief, anger, shock. Most women believed that the only danger seemed to be in being a main speaker, but some maintained that from now on, they'd only go to women's meetings. Emily felt a grim resolve. She fingered Luz' card. Go ahead with tonight, or beg off, claiming to be too upset? Go ahead.

By 5:00 Wednesday, Emily was ready. She wore a loose shirt in royal blue with her white pants and blue hoop earrings. Her makeup was subdued. She slid the casserole into the oven and relaxed, knowing that everything was set from her end.

She took a diet soda and Beaton out to the patio and whiled away the hour, periodically asking herself if she had forgotten anything. No, all preparations were made. Her landlady stuck her head out the window.

"You look nice, Emily. Going out or entertaining?"

"Having someone over. Okay if we use the patio?"

"Of course. I'll just be indoors listening to music. You have fun."

At 6:00, Ed rang the bell and she let him in. His lanky legs were encased in jeans and he wore a pin-striped shirt tucked in. He was carrying a sheath of roses.

"How beautiful. Let me get some water for those."

Emily found a vase and set the flowers on the table. She took the casserole out of the oven.

"We can eat now, or this will stay hot if you'd like something to drink first."

"What have you got?"

"Diet soda, cranberry juice, sparkling water."

"I'll have a water; that sounds good."

"Shall we go out to the patio?"

"Sure."

They sipped and made small talk. Emily was unaccountably nervous, and she noticed that Ed had a tic by the corner of his mouth.

"I'm actually not used to entertaining guys. In fact, I haven't dated in eighteen years."

"I'm honored to be the first."

"I don't want dinner to get cold. Shall we move back in?"

"Sure. Whatever you say."

Emily served up the chops, rice, and salad.

"This is delicious. I love pork."

"It's an old recipe I got from my mother."

"It's wonderful. So, this is a charming place. First time I've been inside. Have you lived here long?"

"About ten years now. I rent the cottage and share the patio with the owner. She's an elderly lady who doesn't get out much, so it works out fine."

"May I help you with the dishes?"

"Oh no. Guests don't work. I'll just stack them in the kitchen. We've got ice cream for dessert, but I thought we could wait awhile and have it in the living room."

"Sounds good. Do I smell coffee?"

"I made us a pot of decaf. Want a cup?"

"Love one."

They took their coffee and settled in, Ed in the armchair and Emily on the couch. Well, it was now or never.

"So Ed, tell me about Molly and Virginia and now Laura."

He spread his hands. "Well, I didn't know them very well. I only heard them speak twice, once when I auditioned them, as it were, and once when they came to the Friday night meeting. Who's Laura?"

"And these auditions?"

"I always like to vet the speakers, to make sure they can hold their own in front of a group that size. Not everyone can, you know. Sometimes they freeze."

Emily took a deep breath. "And once you got them, how did you do it?"

Ed gazed at her steadily. "You really want to know?"

"I really do."

"It all starts with charm. I can be very charming when I want to."

"I noticed."

"Well, with Molly, I came up to her in the parking lot. With Virginia, I called her after I'd dropped her off at home. Laura I'd been dating. There I had to improvise. What with no more women Friday night, I had to use her Tuesday night speaking engagement.

With all three, I said I'd gotten a desperate call from a drunk and needed someone to go with me on a twelve-step call."

So Elaine's hunch had been right.

"How did you get them to drink alcohol?"

"I got them in a choke hold, which cuts off the oxygen to the brain so the person passes out. Then I poured the alcohol down their throats. I knew in advance what kind of liquor had been their favorite. I thought that was a unique touch. Then I stripped them and attacked them with a baseball bat."

"Why?"

"Why did I do it? I'm the one who put them behind the podium, who gave them the glory. So I was the one who took them down."

"Why only women?"

"Women, sorry to say, are easier to subdue. Then too, it's a woman I was mad at."

"Your ex-wife?"

"My mother. When I was growing up, my mother and stepfather were terrible drunks. He used to beat me up something awful, using a bat, and she did nothing to stop him. Nothing. When I was about fourteen, they both got sober. 'We're sorry' is all they had to say to me. They just expected me to be so proud of them for getting sober and to forgive them, as if nothing had happened."

"That was a long time ago."

"I got the idea then, and I bided my time. As far as perfecting the technique though, I had practice. I used to practice on skid row prostitutes. It took some doing to get it down just right."

"So the idea was to humiliate and then kill speakers."

"That's basically it."

"And was I on the list?"

"Of course. Sooner or later. Now it will just have to be sooner rather than later."

Ed lunged. Emily dropped and rolled. The door flew open.

"Police! Freeze!" Luz Gutierrez burst through the door, followed by Fred Hansen. They subdued and cuffed Ed. He looked over at Emily incredulously.

"You asked me to dinner and you were wearing a wire?"

"Got it."

"I have to say, you've got serious trust issues."

Fred read Ed his rights and led him away. Luz stayed to make sure Emily was all right.

"You going to be okay now?"

"Yes. The shaking will stop. Everything came through on the microphone?"

"Loud and clear. We heard it all from the van parked right across the street. Now how about you? Do you want me to call someone?"

"My best friend Marianne might come over, even though it's a working night."

"That would be good."

Indeed, Marianne was willing to come. Luz helped Emily undo the wire and stayed until her friend arrived. She was adamant that Emily, having gone through an ordeal, should not be alone. Emily did not demur.

Epilogue

Marianne came right over. She hugged Emily, introduced herself to Luz, who had waited until she arrived to leave, and carried cups out to the patio while Emily brought the rest of the pot of decaf.

"Weren't you terrifed?"

"Sure, it was scary. Making small talk beforehand was the hardest part, actually. I felt really stilted. Since I knew that the detectives were right outside, though, I felt pretty safe."

"I feel so foolish, encouraging you to go out with Ed. I really thought he had a good program. Alex thought so highly of him."

"How were you to know? He had everyone fooled. He was so active in AA, and he certainly knew how to talk the talk."

"What if you'd been wrong, Emily. What if he'd been innocent? It would have totally ruined the relationship."

"True enough. But I decided I had to risk it. If I'd been wrong, that would have been some colossal amends to make, right?"

"I'll say. So he was stringing you along, taking it nice and easy, and at the same time he was dating Laura. How did he manage that?"

"I go to meetings primarily in Pasadena, South Pasadena, San Marino. She stayed pretty much in Arcadia and West Covina. So our paths were not likely to cross."

"What amazes me the most is that the detectives let you do it."

"It took some persuading. Luz Gutierrez was totally opposed to the idea at first. Then, when I told her I was planning to confront him anyway, with or without back-up, she cleared it with her lieutenant and they got a court order. Laura's murder was the last straw. They knew from talking with her son that she had a boyfriend, but they didn't know who he was."

"So Friday night is safe again. Are you planning to go?"

"Sure. I'll go for the rest of the summer."

Once Marianne left, Emily did up the dishes and put away the leftovers. Oddest dinner party she'd ever given. The casserole served four; there was enough for two more meals. She decided to ask Sue over on Thursday. Talking with Marianne, she'd still been amped up, but now fatigue was catching up to her. After giving fervent thanks, she climbed into bed.

Thursday morning, she called Elaine and filled her in.

"So, you see, you were right about the phony 12-step call as the method."

"Always nice to be right. I notice that you did not run your plan to trap the killer by me, though."

"Sorry about that. I know I tend to go my own way."

Elaine laughed. "That you sure do. But all's well that ends well."

Eddie Park was close enough to walk to, but by 11:00 the sun was really beating down, so Emily chose to drive. She was pleased to see that they had four volunteers this week for set-up. The work went quickly. As usual, Zack came just as they were finishing up. He was bursting with news.

"Word is that the police have made an arrest. It should be all right for women to speak again."

"Glad to hear it. I like the plan of alternating man, woman."

"It must feel good to know that the threat has been removed."

"Yes, it's a big relief."

Lunch was fresh fish, caught and cooked by Fisherman Frank. Summers, he went out several times on big charters and caught as much as he could. Emily enjoyed the meal.

The speaker had come all the way from Torrance. He'd known Dr. Paul and had many good anecdotes of AA history. Emily was thoroughly entertained. After the meeting, she thanked him profusely for making the journey.

"Ah, well. Glad to do it. 'Go to any lengths,' after all."

Upon returning home, she emailed her mother and left a phone message with her father, letting them know that all was well and that the danger had passed. Then it was time for a nap before Sue came over.

"So I'm eating killer leftovers."

"That's about it. Seemed a pity to waste it."

"Well, it's delicious. I'm glad you thought of me. Sometime soon you'll have to come over to my place for a barbecue."

"Absolutely. Just let me know when and where."

"You know what makes me sad about all this? All the children who are left. Molly had a grandchild. Virginia had her partner's kids. Laura had a teenage son."

"Oh yes. He created tremendous damage. Fortunately, Laura had a sister who's able to take in the son, so he won't have to go into foster care."

"At least that's something. When did you begin to suspect Ed?"

"Not until the very end. There were a couple of reasons. For one, he was so proud of his list of speakers, vetting them carefully as if they were his prize possessions. Then too, he was so totally charming. In the literature, killers often put up a really good front."

"I'm just glad you came out of the whole thing alive."

"Believe me, I'm super grateful."

Friday afternoon, Emily called the Hendricks, wanting to tie up all loose ends. The pastor went home for lunch, so she was able to speak with both of them. They rejoiced and thanked God for a successful resolution.

Friday night. Speaker meeting? Why not. Emily had no sooner arrived than Tom Carney came bustling up to her, waving a sheet of paper.

"Say, there. I'm trying to reconstruct Ed's list of speakers. One thing about him, he did find good ones. Now, I see he has you penciled in for the end of August. Any chance you can still make it?"

"I'd be happy to, Tom."

He put a check by her name. "Good, good. I've called almost everyone else. So it looks like we've got the summer all set. Nice to get back to normal."

The general mood at the meeting was one of exuberant release. Whereas people had been tense and afraid, now they could relax into security again. Newcomers were back to flirting; oldtimers were back to giving counsel and enjoying themselves. Emily spotted Marianne over by the coffee urn, giving her number to an eager new prospect. She strolled over to greet her.

"Feels good, doesn't it? Back on an even keel."

"Yep. Things are running smoothly again. And now you have the rest of the summer to relax and enjoy. What will you do with yourself after your big adventure?"

"I thought I might write up the murders. Make it a book by Nancy D."

"Good plan. Use a pseudonym, remain anonymous. Where'd you get the name?"

"It's short for Nancy Drew."

Also available from PublishAmerica

THE MAGIC COTTAGE
by Hannah Greer

Eight-year-old twins Asa and Prentiss Fallmark are spending the summer with their grandparents. Grammy and Papa set a goal for the month-long vacation: the twins are to investigate and stretch their imaginations without the use of television, electronic gadgets, or radio. Each morning, the siblings board their "imagination transporter" at the top of a hill adjacent to their grandparents' home. The twins have remarkable adventures in the land they call Serendipity where they "build" the magic cottage and meet many new friends who provide them with mystical gifts. The children become integral parts of exciting experiences in which they must use their minds and imaginations to overcome conflict. Scientific studies they learned in school develop special meanings as they explore Serendipity. Hints occur throughout the story that the grandparents know more about Serendipity than the children realize. Could it be that Grammy and Papa have magical powers?

Paperback, 132 pages
5.5" x 8.5"
ISBN 1-60672-190-9

About the author:

Hannah Greer has embraced writing since she was a child. As an educator and founder of an experiential school, she guided underachievers to utilize their imaginations. Teaming up with her illustrator sister, Tica Greer, a new series of books based on exciting adventures, *The Velvet Bag Memoirs*, has been born.

Available to all bookstores nationwide.
www.publishamerica.com

Also available from PublishAmerica
HOTEL TRANSYLVANIA
by Michael T.G. Yepes

This is a novel about exiles, refugees and immigrants. The time is the early 18th century; the scene is Paris. The location is a gambling establishment of dubious reputation—the Hotel de Transylvania. Situated on the Seine embankment, across the Louvre, a group of Hungarian expatriates support themselves on their good looks, charm, guile and political connection. This establishment is run by the grey eminence of the Abbé Brenner, under the protection of the exiled Prince of Transylvania. This is the story of the denizens of that hotel from 1713 to 1717. It is about being a foreigner, yet crafty and adaptable; it is about entering a new social environment, and succeeding or failing in Europe's most glamorous and exciting city. And it is also a reflection on a society that was rapidly emerging from the rigid rule of Louis XIV to the expanding freedoms under the Orléans regency. In the background, there is the still-smouldering conflict between the Jesuits and Jansenists. The sacred and the profane, constantly juxtaposed and confronting each other, in an environment of fabulous wealth and painful poverty—and four young men absorbing it all.

Paperback, 210 pages
5.5" x 8.5"
ISBN 1-4241-5219-4

About the author:

Michael T.G. Yepes was born in Budapest, Hungary, and came to the U.S. in 1956, after the Hungarian Revolution. He had received his secondary and college education in Budapest, and graduated from Medical School in San Francisco. A life-long interest in history and literature lead him to the California Missions, and eventually to the Jesuits on the California Peninsula. M.T.G. Yepes is married and lives with his wife in West Los Angeles. They have three adult children and 7 grandchildren.

Available to all bookstores nationwide.
www.publishamerica.com